Other John Cuddy novels by Jeremiah Healy

Blunt Darts
The Staked Goat
So Like Sleep
Swan Dive
Yesterday's News
Right to Die
Shallow Graves

Published by POCKET BOOKS

YESTERDAY'S NEWS

Jeremiah Healy

POCKET BOOKS

New York   London   Toronto   Sydney   Tokyo   Singapore

POCKET BOOKS, a division of Simon & Schuster Inc.
1230 Avenue of the Americas, New York, NY 10020

Copyright © 1989 by Jeremiah Healy
Cover art copyright © 1990 Sonja Lamut

All rights reserved, including the right to reproduce
this book or portions thereof in any form whatsoever.
For information address Harper & Row Publishers Inc.,
10 East 53rd Street, New York, NY 10022

ISBN: 0-671-69584-3

First Pocket Books printing September 1990

10 9 8 7 6 5 4 3 2

POCKET and colophon are registered trademarks of
Simon & Schuster Inc.

Printed in the U.S.A.

For Larry Ashmead

ONE

♦

Elie said, "Now, you lift, John. Take two seconds, two seconds. Good. Now lower. Take four. Remember, count of two when you lift, count of four when you lower."

"Right."

"Now again. Two up . . . four down. Try to hold it for one second at the top. That's it."

This time I didn't answer him.

"Again. Two . . . one . . . four. You're jerking the weight a little. Try to be smoother."

I tried.

"Two. Better. One. Now four. Except for the pause at the top, the muscles respond better when you lift and lower in a continuous motion."

Six more repetitions.

"Okay, stop. That was good, John, very good."

Kneading the knots just above my knees, I looked

up at the mirrored wall reflecting Elie standing and me sitting, strapped into the leg machine.

He said, "How do the quadriceps feel?"

"Like I just had surgery on them."

Elie laughed the way they did before the time of troubles in his native Lebanon. "That's normal. This Nautilus equipment, it tells you about muscles you haven't used for a while."

Trim and tanned, he shifted a clipboard to his other hand, penciling an entry on the chart he'd begun for me. "John Francis Cuddy. You're what, about six-three?"

"Little under."

"One-ninety?"

"Little over."

"Guy as big as you and your age, you're in pretty good shape already. What kind of work do you do?"

"Private investigator."

"Really?"

"It's not like they paint it on TV. For conditioning, I've mostly been running."

"What kind of distance?"

"Maybe three to five miles, three times a week."

"That's okay. Don't have to do more unless you're in training for something." He secured the pencil under the clip. "Next machine is the leg curl."

I lay flat on my stomach, knees just off the edge of the long, horizontal slat. I gripped the handles under the slat for stability, hooking the backs of my ankles under the padded rollers.

"You're going to use the hamstrings here like they were biceps, to bring the roller up, touching it to your buttocks if you can. Try it."

I did. "Too much weight, Elie."

"I'll drop it ten pounds." He fiddled at the front of the machine. "Now try."

I was able to do eight repetitions, faltering halfway up on the ninth.

"Good," he said, writing it down. "We go for twelve reps at the given weight each time, but as long as you can do at least eight, don't decrease the weight. Force your muscles to failure each time, each machine."

Elie put me through seven more machines, several of which had two functions. By the end, my tee shirt was drenched and draining into the elastic band of my gym shorts. He guided me to the front desk.

"We keep the air-conditioning on low. Better to work up a good sweat than risk a bad chill."

"I can believe the sweat part."

He reached beneath the desk and took out a rate sheet. "You get used to it. The designer of the system, he made each machine different, to make each muscle perform the way he wants. You come in three, four times a week. Always give yourself at least forty-eight hours' recovery time for the muscles between work-outs. A lot of runners tell me they work out better if they run first, then do Nautilus." He positioned the rate sheet so that I could see the different periods and payments covered.

I said, "How about six months to start with?"

"Fine, but a year saves you money. Also, we can maybe work out a family plan. You married?"

I thought of Beth and almost said "widowed." Instead, I completed the paperwork as a single and went into the locker room to shower and change.

Elie's facility is three blocks from the condo I was renting in Boston's Back Bay. Nancy Meagher was coming over for dinner that night. I had two hours until a 2:00 P.M. client appointment at the office, so I stopped at one of the high-quality, higher-priced yuppie emporiums on the way home.

I picked up a pound and a half of filet mignon, a beefsteak tomato, and a fresh French baguette. At the cash register, the clerk rang it in and then whistled softly. "That'll be $25.28."

"You're kidding."

"Nope. It's the filet. Really runs it up."

I handed him three tens. He said, "I'll give you the receipt. So that your friends will believe you really paid that much for their dinner."

"Don't bother. *I* was here and I don't believe it."

Walking back to the condo, I felt loose and relaxed, as though I'd just had a soothing massage. I expected significant stiffness the next day.

The parking lot behind the building looked empty without my Fiat 124 in it. I hadn't liked the way the steering was fading, and the engine was running rough, so I had taken it over to Arnie's Garage that morning.

Retrieving my mail from the community lockbox in the brownstone's foyer, I climbed the stairs to the second-floor unit owned by a doctor on a two-year residency in Chicago. The apartment was bright, even in the deflected sunshine, thanks to seven stained-glass windows across its southern wall. My landlord's teak and burlap furniture lent a classy yet homey touch to the place.

I put the filet in the refrigerator and tried to straighten things a little. I'm more an Oscar than a Felix, but this was going to be Nancy's first time at my place, and I was nervous about her reaction to it. Or, to be honest, my reaction to her staying over.

The telephone rang. I sank into the couch and answered it. "John Cuddy."

"John, this is Arnie."

"Great. You have my estimate?"

"Yeah. You sitting down?"

"Yes."

"Better lie down."

"Arnie . . ."

"Fifteen hundred."

"What?"

"A one and a five with—"

"What the hell can be that wrong with a fourteen-year-old car?"

"Jesus, John, with a fourteen-year-old car there ain't much that's still right. You got a steering column with arthritis, an engine block with the emphysema there . . ."

When Doctor Doom finished his list, I said, "What are my options?"

"None. Scrap the Fiat's what I'd do."

"Arnie, where's your soul?"

"You want soul, soul costs fifteen hundred. You want brains, bag the coupe and get something that'll last you."

"Any suggestions?"

"Well . . . yeah. I got this Honda Prelude, 'eighty-two. Last year of their earlier model. Silver with red seats, only thirty thousand miles on it. Stockbroker out in Lincoln used it as his station car, but the silly fuck can't drive a shift anymore on account of he cracked his leg skiing in Utah last month."

"Skiing in May?"

"Yeah. Deserves it, don't he?"

"How much for the Fiat?" I said.

"You mean the Honda?"

"No, I mean how much will you give me as trade-in on the Fiat?"

"Trade-in? Tell you what, I won't charge you a dime for diagnosing this terminally ill shitbox of yours I got standing in the corner of my garage, and I'll give you the Prelude for three and a half."

"Thirty-five hundred dollars?"

"That's right. It's mint, oughta be in a glass case somewheres instead—"

"I'll have to get back to you, Arnie."

"By tomorrow, okay? I gotta get your Typhoid Mary outta here before it infects the cars around it."

"By tomorrow."

I took out the checkbook. The infusion of cash from my old apartment being burned was down to six thousand and change. God knew what the jump in insurance might be for the "new" car. The rent due on the condo and the check I'd just given Elie would wipe out the money coming in from existing cases.

I hoped the potential client at 2:00 P.M. was solvent. If not, I might have to return the filet.

"John Cuddy?"

I looked up from my desk at the woman in the doorway. I'd left the door open to encourage cross-ventilation from the two windows behind me in the office, my air conditioner being on the fritz again.

"Ms. Rust, come in."

About five-four in low heels, she wore a gray skirt and a blue blazer. Her hair was light brown and would have been long if she didn't part it in the center and pull it back into a bun. Her eyeglasses were big and round, her shoulder bag the size of a briefcase. As she approached me, I could see she used a little too much

6

makeup, as though she were twenty-five and insecure trying very hard to look thirty-five and confident.

We shook hands, and she sat across from me. "Professor Katzen said you were a good detective."

It was hard for me to imagine anyone calling Mo Katzen at the *Herald* anything but a dinosaur reporter, but I said, "I hope I'll be able to help you."

"Did he . . . did he tell you why I need help?"

"No. He just telephoned and left a message that a Jane Rust might be contacting me. Other than your call setting up this appointment, I don't know anything."

She nodded, as though the absence of prior information meant she could somehow speak more freely. "I'm a reporter, Mr. Cuddy. On the Nasharbor *Beacon*. Are you familiar with it?"

Her accent said central midwest, but she pronounced the seaport like a lifelong resident. Nush-*ar*-burr.

"I don't think I've ever seen the paper. Nasharbor's just south of Fall River, right?"

"Between Fall River and the Rhode Island border. Population 125,000, most of them conservative, working class, and Catholic. Portuguese fishing poor, Irish industrial poor."

Rust spoke in a podium voice, as though she expected me to challenge her demographics.

I said, "Does the paper figure into this?"

"Yes and no. Do you know much about newspapers?"

"Just through Mo—Professor Katzen."

"Well, the *Beacon* is a typical small city daily with typical attitudes about who to protect and expose. It doesn't like its reporters looking into certain things."

"Like what?"

"Like pornography."

"Pornography. Not pleasant, but also not illegal."

She sucked in her cheeks and said, "How about kiddie porn, Mr. Cuddy. That strikes even the Supreme Court as illegal."

"Kiddie porn in Nasharbor. Is this what we're talking about here?"

"Look, do you want to hear what my problem is or don't you?"

"I'm sorry. Why don't you tell me without my interrupting."

Rust took a deep breath and broke eye contact. "About three months ago, I was covering a Saturday night. They give the younger . . . the newer reporters the weekends. There was a state police raid just outside the city limits. The staties turned up some videocassettes and 'photo essays.' The weekend editor was swamped, and I volunteered to go out on the story. I interviewed one of the men they arrested, and he told me that a Nasharbor cop was on the take and had protected the clearinghouse for all the stuff."

When she didn't continue, I said, "Did the *Beacon* ever run your story?"

She laughed, a bitter edge on it. "Sure. They ran a story under my byline about how the state police had busted up a ring of porn peddlers at the outskirts of Nasharbor and wasn't it wonderful that all this filth hadn't penetrated the best little city on the eastern seaboard."

"What about the corruption angle?"

"They buried it. Said they wouldn't print it unless I revealed my confidential source."

That didn't sound right. "The paper wouldn't run the story without the name of the guy you talked to in it?"

"No, no. The editor wouldn't run the story without me telling him, that editor, the name of the source."

I watched her for a minute.

"What's the matter?" she said.

"I guess I'm thinking that if I'm the editor involved, I might want to know your source's name before I let fly at the local cops."

The cheeks imploded again. "Maybe I'm wasting my time here."

"Ms. Rust, I just don't see where I fit in."

She toned down. "He's dead."

"Who?"

"My source. They killed him to shut him up."

"Who killed him?"

Her eyes glowed fanatically. "The cops, who else?"

Uh-oh. "Ms. Rust, cops don't—"

"I am wasting my time."

"Ms. Rust, hear me out, okay? Reciprocal courtesy?"

She folded her arms but remained rigid in the chair. Rust was going to hear me out alright. She just wasn't going to listen. I decided to give it a try anyway.

"Cops don't have to kill people like your source to shut them up. Guys like your source are usually involved in action the cops know about. It's risky to kill somebody, especially when there's a motive to kill. It's a lot safer just to pressure the guy, tell him if he rolls over on us, we turn up some new 'evidence' and nail him for something that sends him away for heavy time. Like maybe to Walpole State Prison or Cedar Junction or whatever the hell they call it now, where all sorts of bad things happen to guys who rat on other people."

She smiled sarcastically. "You said 'we.'"

"I'm sorry?"

"When you were talking about cops just now, you used 'we' and 'us.' You identify with them, don't you?"

"I was military police, and I've worked with all kinds of law enforcement over the years. I suppose I do identify with them. That doesn't mean I think they're all good scouts. It does mean I don't easily see even the bad scouts doing something stupid."

She unfolded her arms and hunched forward. "Look, Mr. Cuddy, I've gotten no support on this. None! From anyone! My editor thinks I'm a loose cannon, I can't sleep, my personal life's a mess. All I want to do, all I ever wanted to do, is be a good reporter, and now you won't help me either."

Rust turned sideways, snatching off the glasses with her left hand and clamping the right to her face to dam the tears. I opened three drawers before I found the Kleenex box I knew I'd bought weeks ago. I pushed it toward her. She crumpled one, then came back for another. The tears and tissues savaged her mascara.

Putting her glasses back on, she said, "I need somebody to look into the man's death, Mr. Cuddy. I understand it'll cost money, but I owe him that much."

She looked up at me with the defiant dignity of a high school girl who doesn't have a date for the prom but decides to go anyway. Wrecked makeup and all, it gave her a surprising air of attraction.

"Ms. Rust—"

"Please, call me Jane."

"Jane. I'm not saying I'll accept the case. Police anywhere take a dim view of a private investigator poking into a killing. But I'm willing to hear more first if you're willing to tell it."

She nodded. "The head porno guy is named

Gotbaum. I can write all this out for you with first names and addresses and all. My source . . . my source's name was Coyne, Charlie Coyne. He was kind of a messenger, carrying some of the stuff. He . . . they found him in an alley behind one of the bars in the part of town . . . the part we call The Strip. Kind of like your Combat Zone up here."

"Topless bars, peep shows, that kind of thing?"

"Right, right. When the city fathers, and I emphasize the gender, decided that it would cost more to close them down than hem them in, a decision was made to sacrifice three blocks down near the cannery. It was called The Strip long before I ever came to town."

"When was that?"

"When?"

"When you came to town."

"Oh, about two years ago. I worked in Florida, then South Carolina, then New Jersey before I came up here."

I thought it sounded like a lot of stops for someone so young, but I let it go. "How was Coyne killed?"

Rust bit her lip, and then I thought the tears might be back on the way. "Knifed. And robbed. Hagan said Charlie was mugged by a derelict and closed the book on it."

"Hagan?"

"He's the detective captain. In line for chief."

"And you don't believe him because . . ."

She regained a little fire. "I don't believe him because his ex-partner is a guy named Schonstein, or 'Schonsy,' as he is affectionately called." Rust made the last sound like the deepest insult one could inflict. "And, surprise, surprise, guess who the cop is that Coyne told me was on the take?"

"Schonstein."

"Right. But not Schonsy."

"I don't get you."

"The cop with his hand out is Detective Mark Schonstein. Schonsy's son. Hagan's old partner's son. Smell anything now?"

"Schonsy Senior still on the force?"

"Retired. Disability pension a while ago."

"And you figure one of the cops killed Coyne to keep him from . . ."

"From talking to me."

"But he'd already talked to you, right? The night of the raid, I mean?"

"Yes, but I kept after him on it. I wanted to have a story so well documented that even the cops couldn't sweep it under the rug. And if my editor wouldn't run it, I'd find somebody who would."

"How did the cops know that Coyne was your source?"

"I don't know. That's one of the things I need you to find out."

When I didn't go on, Rust fidgeted. Finally I said, "Who did you tell, Jane?"

She shook her head.

"Come on. How am I supposed to find the leak if you won't—"

"I can't, I just can't! I have to know if one of them . . . I have to know without telling you. It probably wasn't even professional to tell. . . . Look, if I was . . . if Charlie was betrayed that way, I want to know you found it out independently. Don't you see?"

"I see that you didn't want your editor to know the name of your source, but that you did tell others. If

12

you don't tell me who the possibilities are, my hands are pretty much tied."

"The people I told wouldn't. . . . They couldn't have told the police about Charlie. I'd feel worse than I do now if I hired you and you made them feel like I suspected them. Besides, I'm sure the cops found out Charlie was my source some other way."

"Well, would Charlie have told anyone?"

Suddenly Rust dipped her head forward, middle fingers rotating gently at the temples like a cocktail lounge mentalist going into her act. "I'm sorry, it's just that I have a splitting headache."

"I think I have some aspirin."

She shook her head again. "Can't. I mean, I can't abide pills. Probably psychosomatic, but I can't swallow anything medicinal, not even those little cold things. I throw up."

"I think they have—"

She cut me off by saying, "I've got to get back. I'm supposed to be working on a series about redevelopment, and this real estate guy who's getting more than he's paying for. Speaking of which . . ." She began rummaging through her shoulder bag. ". . . here, let me give you a check."

"Jane, I haven't said I'd take you on yet."

Rust pushed toward me a pale blue draft with the spidery imprint of a sailing ship. She already had filled in the date, my name, and her signature. "The proverbial blank check."

"Jane—"

"And this is my business card, with my home number."

"I won't accept a blank check."

"What's your daily rate?"

"Three hundred. Plus expenses, which would mean travel, meals, and hotel down there if I did take your case."

I hoped the amount would discourage her. It didn't.

She entered "$900." and "Nine hundred and no cents" on the appropriate lines and got up to leave. "Three days' worth. This way you can think about it and still have to get back to me. Good reporters make people get back to them."

I spent the next two hours catching up on paperwork. I focused on one item in particular. The police commissioner had lifted my permit to carry a concealed weapon because of a failure to report my gun being stolen. I was told on the sly that if I submitted a second request through headquarters on Berkeley Street, the permit would be reinstated.

I kept Jane Rust's check and card, paper-clipped together, on top of the in-box. That forced me to think about her. I really didn't want the case. I really didn't want to spend a week or so living out of a motel in a decaying industrial city with a stinking harbor. And I especially didn't want to make cops there overly eager to roust me for looking into one of their own.

On the other hand, I wasn't going to be a private investigator very long if I had to rely on public transportation to get around. And there was one person within walking distance who might tell me whether Ms. Rust was a client who'd bind.

TWO

"Twenty dollars, John, twenty dollars. Can you believe it?"

"That's steep, Mo."

"Steep? Steep? I'll give you steep, alright." Mo Katzen squared his stubby shoulders, the too-wide tie riding like a scarf beneath the unbuttoned vest to a suit jacket I'd never seen him wear in all the years I'd known him. He ran a hand through his snowy hair and then shook the fire-orange parking violation at me like a medicine man with a gourd rattle. "Time was a citizen could feed a family of four on twenty a week. Of course, time was a citizen could leave his car at the curb in his own city without a RESIDENT PARKING sticker, too."

"Mo, I need—"

"You got one of those?"

"One of what?"

"Those. Those parking decal things."

"Yes."

"You're a traitor to your roots, John."

"I'm sorry, Mo."

"Goddamnest idea." Mo spun the ticket down onto his desk. I wasn't sure whether the surface of the desk was metal or wood, since I'd never seen it through the town dump of sandwich wrappers, Red Sox programs, almanacs, *Playbills,* and probably Mo's own high school yearbook. "Imagine, the Athens of the Atlantic restricting parking to 'Residents Only.'"

"An outrage."

"Mild, John, too mild. Granted, I should have my head examined for even trying to drive into Yuppiedom over by you, but I got invited to a dinner, and I'm not about to pay ten bucks for two hours in one of those private lots."

"And not many of them left."

"Of course not. If there were, the developers couldn't get their price for selling the spaces behind the condo buildings. You know what a space goes for now?"

I decided not to mention the one I rented from my landlord. "No."

"Forty to fifty grand. For an eight-by-twenty table of tar that you couldn't fit a decent-sized car into. Assuming Detroit made decent-sized cars anymore. Which if they did they couldn't sell, because everybody's buying these foreign jobs. You ever see a foreign car in Southie when you were growing up?"

"No, Mo. South Boston was pretty much true blue."

"Bet your ass. Not in Chelsea either. The Irish and the Jews were proud to be in this country. For that

16

matter, you never even saw a Fiat over in the North End, did you?"

"Not that I can—"

"No, no, of course you didn't. All the neighborhoods back then bought American. Now they're calling them 'imported,' you know. Not 'foreign' anymore but 'imported,' like that justifies the king's ransom you gotta pay for them and the whack you give the trade deficit when the dealer negotiates the check, but who cares, right? Tell me this, how the hell you gonna depend on a car you couldn't communicate with the guys who built it?"

"Communicate?"

"Talk with them, for God's sake. How you gonna know if a Yugo's built right, huh? You don't have a next-door neighbor or a guy dating your sister works in a factory on them. You got instead some preppy fraternity president telling you on a television commercial costs a hundred grand a minute how great the little boxes are, but you never get to talk to a guy who builds one."

"You could talk to a mechanic, and I think Ford and GM buy some time on the tube now and—"

"Speaking of a hundred grand." Mo reached for a comatose cigar on the corner of his half-opened top drawer. A good sign that he was winding down. "You know that's what one of them goes for now, don't you?" He lit the cigar with a war memorial lighter as big as a softball.

I said, "A Yugo?"

"No, no. A parking space."

"I thought you said fifty?"

"John, you gotta pay attention here. Fifty just gets you an outdoor space where you gotta contend with the snow and the soot. You want a roof over the little fucker's head, you gotta go a hundred."

"That seems—"

"I just read it. In our new 'Downtown' section, the Sunday supplement that's supposed to win us over all the yuppies I can't stand who've done this to the city in the first place. A 'garage condo' now starts at one hundred grand cash money. Can you imagine that?"

"I sure can't."

"And we're not talking your *own* little garage either, my friend. We're talking one measured slot under a leaky pipe on the third floor of a place looks like Michael Caine's gonna gun down a CIA agent before midnight."

"Mo, I wonder if I—"

"Yep, it's either shell out the long yard for a condo garage space, or leave your little Yugo out on the street. I was mad about this ticket until I passed this one car, old beat-up Mazda, got seven or eight of them tucked under the one wiper still attached. Know what the guy had on his bumper?"

"No."

"Guy's got this sticker, says METER MAIDS EAT THEIR YOUNG. I love it."

"May as well be hanged for a sheep as a lamb."

"What?"

"I said—"

"I heard what you said. Who the hell was talking about livestock here?"

"Mo, it's just an—"

"You know, I gotta lot of work to do before deadline. I can't spend the whole afternoon bringing you back on track like this."

"I know, Mo, and I appreciate it. I'm here about a client you referred to me. Jane Rust."

Mo took a deep drag on the cigar, blew a perfect smoke ring, then another. "What did you think?"

"I met with her today, and I thought I'd come see you, find out what I might have on my hands."

"This Rust. Mid-twenties, kind of mousy, nervous?"

I felt a little ping. "You don't know her."

"I know her, I just don't *know* her, you know?"

"You lost me."

Mo knocked some ashes into his drawer. "Couple of years ago, editor here got me a job teaching adjunct, a journalism school crosstown. This Rust was in one of my classes. Or so she said on the phone."

"She called you Professor Katzen with me."

"Hah." Mo set down the cigar. "Professor Katzen. Yeah, she would, she's the one I'm thinking of."

"She telephoned you?"

"Yeah. She needed an investigator to nose around Nasharbor. Somebody who wasn't already wired into the big boys down there."

"She tell you why?"

"No. You gonna?"

"No. Statute says I can't. But I would like to know this—you figure her for a conspiracy nut?"

Mo stuck the cigar back into his mouth and spoke around it. "Can't help you there. I just don't remember her much. Only saw her for a couple of hours on maybe ten Tuesdays two years ago. She asked some questions, gave some answers, barely stuck in my mind."

When I didn't reply, Mo said, "What I'm saying is, you don't owe me anything on this. You want to take her case, you take it. You don't, no offense on my part."

I got up. "Thanks, Mo."

Reaching the door, I heard him punch in a telephone number and say, "Parking Bureau? Listen, we gotta talk here."

Walking back to the condo, I averted my eyes from the traitorous, but still empty, parking space. Upstairs, I showered and shaved for the second time that day, the face protesting that it was too soon to be scraped again. I used styptic pencil to stanch the blood, and aftershave to wipe off the white, powdery residue. Pulling on a Ralph Lauren Polo shirt and Reebok sport shorts for Nancy, I decanted a bottle of red wine and chopped some fresh spinach, proscuitini, and cheddar cheese into a simple salad.

The downstairs buzzer sounded. From the staircase, I could see her through the second of two glass-paneled doors. Lustrous black hair, charcoal suit, white ruffled blouse still looking fresh after a tough day litigating for the Suffolk County district attorney's office downtown.

I opened the door, and the hand that wasn't carrying her briefcase came out from behind her back. A mixed bouquet of flowers.

"Pity I just pawned the Ming vase."

She went up on her toes to kiss me. "Only a Holy Cross grad would consider putting flowers in a Ming vase." The kiss was sweet, a combination of nature and wintergreen Tic Tac.

"Let's continue this upstairs."

Nancy followed me. "Your buzzer system broken?"

"No. After the nurse was raped and murdered on Commonwealth, we disconnected the door latch part of it."

"Welcome to Back Bay."

"Sorry."

"I'm sorry, too. It's just been that kind of day."

At the apartment door, I motioned for Nancy to step past me over the threshold. "Well, what do you think?"

She moved her head slowly around the apartment, taking in the polished oak-front fireplace, the lavender windows, and the Scandinavian Design furnishings. "I knew I should have gone to medical school."

Nudging her toward the couch, I went to the kitchen. "Wine or hard stuff?"

"What's the wine?"

"Robert Mondavi, 1982 Cabernet Sauvignon."

"You're impressing me."

"Wait'll you see the receipt for the entree."

"Maybe half a glass of the wine, John."

I poured us both the same amount and carried the carafe and long-stemmed crystal on a Fanueil Hall Memorial tray.

Nancy smiled up at me. "After the day I've had, this is really wonderful."

Putting the tray on the coffee table, I said, "Want to tell me about it?"

The smile faded. "Only briefly."

"Only briefly" stretched into forty minutes and a second round of wine. Three guys in a local rock band fancied a cocktail waitress during a gig at one of the student madhouses in Allston. She didn't return quite the groupie fascination they'd come to expect, so they waited for her in their van afterward. Four hours later, they dumped her behind a boarded-up building in the Combat Zone.

Nancy said, "It was her mother made her go to the police the next day. Fortunately, she drew an officer who cared, and he triggered the Rape Unit."

"Any physical evidence left?"

"Yes and no. The victim had bathed and douched herself for a couple of hours, which pretty well eliminated the semen and hair possibilities. But there were plenty of bruises, and a bartender who corroborates her story of the guys hitting on her beforehand."

"Where are you now?"

"I just finished my direct of the bartender. Tomorrow, they'll cross him, then probably put their own clients on the stand."

"That's pretty unusual, isn't it?"

"In most criminal cases, yes. But not in rape. Especially not in group rapes like this one. These guys aren't contesting that she was in the van and had intercourse with them. In fact, they bragged about it to their manager afterward. No, they're claiming consent, but they lost their motion to have her prior sexual behavior come in as an exception to the rape shield statute, so it pretty well leaves their word against hers and her physical condition, backed up by photographs at the district station the next day."

"They have any priors?"

"No. Which makes them a lot harder to impeach. But I was watching them while we impaneled the jury. They're cocky, probably figuring the publicity they're getting will increase their name recognition for the future. I think that'll come across as guilty arrogance, not innocent righteousness, once I have a shot at them."

We ate dinner, my filet mignon garnering almost the level of praise the price tag warranted. The wine was just right, and Nancy put some symphonic music on the stereo system that the doctor couldn't bear moving from the custom-built cabinet next to the hearth. We lay back, slanted in toward each other on the couch, sipping the last of the wine.

"I like where you live, John."

"It's grown on me the last couple of hours."

"Thanks to the company?"

"Mustn't fish for compliments, counselor."

She slid her hand up to my neck, flicking and tugging gently on the roots right at the hairline.

I looked into her eyes, blue and wide-spaced, the freckles that multiplied week by week as the sun scaled higher in the early summer sky. "After the kind of stuff you had to deal with today, I'd understand if you'd rather not tonight."

She moved her head slowly, left to right. "I waited long enough for you, John Cuddy. I'm not about to miss any chances now. And besides, after the kind of stuff I dealt with today, what I'd really like is a night of nice, slow lovemaking, to put sex back where it belongs rather than turn against it." She stood up and walked to the stereo. "I know a lot of this is new for you still, and I don't want to suggest anything radical, but how would you like to make love to music tonight?"

"Good idea."

"Any requests?"

"Well," I said, putting down my glass and coming up behind her, "let's avoid the 'Minute Waltz.'"

I got to a sitting position and picked up the telephone by the third ring. Every muscle was tight but strangely refreshed from the Nautilus workout and being with Nancy. The circulating floor fan blew the sheets against my legs as Nancy groped for an unfamiliar light switch. The luminescent dial on the clock radio read 5:45 A.M.

"Hello?"

"John?"

"Who is this?"

"John, it's Mo, Mo Katzen."

"Mo. What the hell is it?"

"I'm in the newsroom, John. At the *Herald*. One of the guys here just heard from somebody he knows down near Nasharbor."

"What happened?"

"It's the Rust girl. Jane Rust, the reporter. They found her dead in her apartment. Suicide, looks like."

"Shit."

"I thought you oughta know," he said, and hung up.

THREE

How did she die?

"I don't know, Beth." Bending down, I arranged the mums longways to her. There were a few sport fishing boats in the harbor below her hillside, but the people on them looked more involved in basking than baiting and casting. "Preliminary indication is suicide, but I don't have any details."

Were you going to take her case?

"I don't know that, either. Mo Katzen really couldn't vouch for her. She'd just been a student of his years ago. And she struck me as a little . . . high-strung."

High-strung or strung out?

"Good question."

I mean, do you think she was suicidal?

"No." I was surprised to hear myself say that, but it was true. "No, when she left me, I thought she was getting a grip on herself, like talking with me had settled her down. She even gave me a check, which she figured would force me to get back to her."

Which you wouldn't have been able to do if she'd killed herself in the meantime.

"Exactly. Of course, that doesn't mean that something couldn't have pushed her over the edge after she left me yesterday afternoon."

Is it legal to keep her check?

"Getting mercenary?"

You know what I mean. Is it legal for you to go on after she's dead?

"There's nothing in the licensing statute, so Nancy couldn't say for sure. And it's tough for her to advise me when she's technically a government lawyer who's not supposed to be handling private clients."

So what are you going to do?

"First, I'm going to pick up my new car."

What happened to the Fiat?

"Forced retirement. The new one—or at least the newer one—is a Honda Prelude."

From Renault to Fiat to Honda. Does that mean you're moving up in the world?

"At least moving."

What are you going to do about the reporter?

"I'm going to drive down to Nasharbor, stay a few days, and see if I can convince myself that Jane Rust was both wrong and suicidal."

Stay well.

I turned to go.

And John?

"Yes?"

Give Nancy my best.

"I will."

* * *

The trip to Nasharbor was almost a pleasure. After paying for the Prelude at Arnie's and waiting in line at both the Registry of Motor Vehicles and my insurance agency, I took Route 3 to Route 128, and then Route 24 south toward the Narragansett coast. The Fiat had been one of the last cars imported before the catalytic converter–unleaded gas requirements and was a rocketship in its prime. However, the pressure of aging and the demise of leaded premium gas had reduced its acceleration mightily, and the gearshift, despite synchromesh, required double clutching half the time. By comparison, the Honda was smooth as silk and quick as a cat, the fifth gear allowing me to cruise near sixty at only 2,400 rpms. The car also sported a moon roof, retractable electrically, which created the illusion of a convertible provided I didn't turn my head too much.

Nasharbor itself, however, was an end that didn't justify the means. Patch-paved roads with gravel to fill the potholes. Dense, two-decker neighborhoods on hillsides overlooking abandoned mills. Adjacent, vacant lots in moonscape, strewn with washers missing lids, grocery carts without wheels, Ford Falcons and other ancients in random pieces.

Main Street was dominated by old structures of red and yellow brick, dingy and dowdy on blocks leavened by churches, taverns, and the occasional VFW or Moose hall. The displays of retail stores were sparse, as though there were inadequate inventory for both shelves and windows. Their patrons were flabby women in gaudy, mismatched blouses and pants. Outside, skinny men waited in bowling jackets and baseball caps, the crowns reaching too high above the forehead. Three kids with a bag of popcorn threw some at the window of a branch bank, the poor guy sitting inside frowning and wagging his head.

The *Beacon* sign appeared just to the harborside of downtown, but I drove past to the waterfront itself. Dilapidated wooden warehouses lay lengthwise on deteriorating pile and stone wharves. The wharves serviced oily, smoky fishing boats. Many of the boats approached fifty feet in length, painted whatever colors the marine hardware store suffered in overstock and bearing female names like *Marie* and *Tina II*.

I stopped the car for a minute. Some of the fishermen, in port for the first time in probably a week, were hanging the nets to dry or hosing down the decks. Others stripped off the layers of oilskin slicker and sweater needed for warmth on the big water even on a summer's day. Working or changing, they yelled and laughed back and forth in Portuguese. I felt disoriented, marooned in another country.

I turned the key in the ignition and headed back toward the *Beacon*.

"You what?"

"I said I want to see someone about Jane Rust. My name's John Cuddy, and I'm a private investigator from Boston." I showed the woman at the horseshoe reception desk my identification.

She looked at it and shook her head hard enough to nearly dislodge her pilot's headphone and mouthpiece. "I don't know who here could help you."

There were three chairs and a table in a sitting area off to the left. "How about I wait till something occurs to you?"

I sat in one of the chairs and picked up a copy of the previous day's *Beacon* from the table. It was a long form paper like the *Boston Globe* or the *New York Times*. Skimming it, I got the impression of a first section focused on the city, followed by others labeled National, Regional, and Sports. It seemed to have more coverage and articles than I would have thought a local daily could produce.

A new voice said, "What do you want?"

I lowered the paper. A thickset man of forty-five stared down at me. His jowls sagged like the plots on network TV. He wore the pants of a cheap green suit, and a white shirt with a flyaway collar. A K Mart tie was pulled down from his neck, and the sleeves on his shirt were rolled up unevenly.

"My name's John Cuddy. I'm a private investigator and I want to talk about Jane Rust with someone in authority. Are you it?"

"The cops are the authority around here. You want me to call them?"

"Eventually. But you might want me to tell you things before you find out I told them things. Your choice."

His jaw realigned twice before he said, "My name's Arbuckle. I'm managing editor. Come back to my office."

Arbuckle led me through a winding corridor that had computer cables inelegantly braided overhead. We moved into a room measuring a hundred feet wide and twice as long. Pillars rose from the linoleum floor to the high ceiling. The ubiquitous computer cables dropped from ragged holes to most of the fifty or so desks in the area, each with a terminal and screen. An unabridged dictionary lay open on a pedestal stand under a large mural map of Nasharbor's part of the county. There were maybe thirty men and women talking on phones or clacking keyboards, a life-sized Bavarian clock gone mad. From one corner, a police scanner squawked like an electronic parrot. Altogether, it was just about quiet enough to hear a bomb drop.

"The city room," said Arbuckle, as he led me into an interior office whose only window looked out onto the bustle of the people I watched. He closed the door behind me and threw himself into a desk chair without telling me to have a seat. I took one anyway.

"Now," he said, "exactly what do you want here?"

"I understand Jane Rust died last night. I'd like to know what happened."

"Talk to the cops."

"I'm talking to you."

"We think it's kind of bad taste to dwell on suicide. Unless it's somebody prominent, we don't even identify the cause of death in the obit."

"Bad taste."

"That's right."

"She was one of your reporters. One of your own."

"She was . . ." he stopped for a moment, then said, "she came to see you, right?"

"That's right."

"About the confidential source thing, right?"

"Go ahead."

"Well, she probably told you more about it than she told me, but what she told me was screwy enough." Arbuckle rearranged some papers on his desk. It ran Mo Katzen's work space a close second in appearance. "Jane wants to do a story, no, a series of stories, on this kiddie porn thing. I have her on the Redevelopment Authority project, and she isn't giving me shit on that. But Jane had this idea, no, this obsession, that

30

the police here knocked off this scumbag source she had. Only she wouldn't talk about the source at story conference or staff meetings. She wouldn't tell me the guy *was* her source until after he buys the farm, and even then she won't come clean on things that don't make any sense at all."

"Like what?"

"Not the way it works, pal. I gave you a little, now you give me a little. Jane wanted to hire you on her own nickel, that's her business. She's dead now, and I want to know why you're here when she isn't around anymore to pay you."

I considered it. "Because you figure I'm trying to get the paper to foot the bill for keeping me on the investigation."

"Jesus, now why didn't I think of that?"

"At two in the afternoon she wanted me to look into what she believed was a murder conspiracy. Then she ends up dead that night. Sound like the way of nature to you?"

"The way of . . . listen, let me tell you some things, maybe you'll get the point." He took a deep breath, let it out exaggeratedly. "Jane was a lightweight, a beginner who wasn't going to get much better. She had these fantasies, romantic fantasies, of what the newspaper business is like. Exposés, dramatic disclosures, Woodward and Bernstein. Am I getting through to you?"

"She was unrealistic."

"Gold star. She was ridiculous. We hired her on as a Gee-Ay, a general assignment reporter. She'd bounced around too much, paper to paper, for somebody only a couple years out of school. I should have started her in Lifestyles covering store openings and women's stuff, but a couple people liked her, said give her a chance, so I did. Should have had my head examined."

"How'd she get involved in the porno thing if she was so unreliable?"

"Don't remind me. She was covering a Saturday night, skeleton crew. The weekend editor's trying to get lines on two fires and a vehicle fatality, so he sends her out to check on this raid. Then she can't think about anything else but that she's going to protect our fair city from the purveyors of kiddie porn panting at the gates. Obsessive, like I said."

"The source, his name was Charlie Coyne?"

"So I'm told."

"This Coyne character does end up dead."

"This Coyne character was a slug with the life expectancy of a thirteenth-century pickpocket. He hung out down on The Strip. Coyne was lucky to live as long as he did, the kind of people he probably crossed down there."

"How did Jane Rust die?"

"Preliminary says overdose."

"Drugs?"

"Sleeping pills."

I looked at him.

Arbuckle said, "What's the matter, you don't know what sleeping pills do?"

"I know what they do. I also know she said she couldn't take them."

"What?"

"She couldn't swallow pills. Made her sick."

"I don't know anything about that and I could care less. Coyne and Rust are yesterday's news, understand? In fifteen minutes, I got a story conference in

32

the executive editor's office on thirty-six pages of today's news."

"Anybody else here that knew her better than you did?"

Again the exaggerated breath. "Let's make a deal, okay? I give you two names and the rest of the day to poke around here. After that, I see you in the building again, I call the cops to kick your ass off the premises. Seem reasonable to you?"

"What are the names?"

"Malcolm Peete and Liz Rendall. They're both Gee-Ay's and knew Jane as well as anybody could. Okay?"

"Thanks for your consideration."

"Don't mention it. Close the door behind you."

When I pulled the door shut, I felt a tap on my shoulder. I looked into a face badly weathered by the elements, so long as you counted alcohol in with wind and rain. His eyes were bleary, his nose a road map etched in red. The hair was gray, but given the booze his age could have been anywhere from me to sixty.

He said, "You're here about Janey."

"Word travels fast."

"The drums, fellow traveler. The drums tell all."

He didn't seem stiff, just overly metaphorical. "Can you point me toward Malcolm Peete?"

He extended his right hand. "At your service. I plan to get stinking drunk to mourn the poor girl's passing. Care to join me?"

I shook his hand. "Only for one."

"Drink or bottle?" he said as he moved to the closest desk and wangled a tweed sports jacket off the back of its chair.

FOUR
—◆—

"Another?"

"Not just yet, thanks."

Peete shrugged, filling his own glass from the liter of Smirnoff he'd persuaded the bartender to leave with us. It didn't take much persuading in the Watering Hole. Six stools over were two truckers tossing shots-and-beer, sawdust on the floor to soak up any sloshed Bud draft. Wooden bowls of pretzels and peanuts, mixed together, clattered on the oft-wiped old mahogany. No butcher block or ferns in sight.

"They'll be here someday, you know," Peete said.

"Who?"

"The nouveau gentry, who else? There is a limit to which even sweetly slumping Nasharbor can sink before urban renewal rears its ugly, and unwanted, head."

"I haven't seen any warning signs so far."

Peete threw back three fingers of vodka and reached for the bottle again. "You've but to open your eyes to see the waste about to be destroyed around you. Poor Janey was panty-deep in the current efforts before she grew weary of the good fight."

I figured I would have to move pretty quickly to get straight answers from the man. "She said something to me about a development story."

"Yes, development. Or, to be precise, redevelopment. Has an encouraging ring to it, 'redevelopment.' As though society has already tried nobly and failed, but has gleaned something from the initial effort which will improve the next one."

"Which effort are we talking about here?"

"The Harborside Condominiums, Limited. Limited, that is, by the peculiarly polyester vision of its principal partner, one Richard Dykestra, the Horatio Alger of our modest metropolis."

"I haven't seen many likely buyers."

"No, no and you won't, good sir. You see, the buyers aren't going to be trampling each other on their way to the model units. Know why?"

"No."

"Because the economy is wrong for it, the tax climate is wrong for it, and Mr. Dykestra is wrong for it. But that didn't stop the En-Are-ay."

"The . . . ?"

"N-R-A, the Nasharbor Redevelopment Authority. The NRA embraced dear Dykestra's dream and lobbied like demons for an accompanying bond issue to relieve him from the pressures of financial reality."

"And Jane Rust thought something stunk there?"

"Like the cannery in August, my lad. But there are others who can tell you far more about it than I." He paused, running the nail of his index finger down the side of the Smirnoff label. "Coming out of Arbuckle's office back at the *Beacon,* you asked for me specifically. Flattering, but why was that?"

"Arbuckle told me you knew Jane as well as anyone."

Peete smiled ruefully. "He was just trying to get rid of us both. You're a new and hopefully temporary nuisance for him. I'm an old and rather permanent one."

"You've been with the paper a long time?"

"Only seven years, and only the last four under Arbuckle. But while he has the power to hire and fire most of us, I enjoy a rather charmed employment existence. I served in Korea with the dead son of the now nearly senile owner of the rag. When I happened upon some alcohol-induced reverses some time ago, I happily remembered that connection, and my resumé was received with open arms by our publisher, to the immediate and continuing consternation of all responsible for producing a decent paper."

"So Arbuckle's stuck with you, and he was just killing two birds with one stone in sending me after you."

"Yes, in that I'm sure that was his motive. No, in that I probably can in fact advance you in your quest. What exactly is your quest, by the way?"

Peete had put away at least half the liter already, but he was still surprisingly in control of mind and mouth.

I said, "Jane talk with you about her confidential source?"

"Ah, of course. The late, lamented Mr. Coyne. She believed our brothers in blue eradicated him to cover up some corruption scandal, correct?"

"Correct."

"My lad, I'm afraid our Janey had some misconceptions about reporting in general and the police here in particular."

"Like what?"

"Well," Peete scoffed two more ounces of eighty proof, "let's begin with reporting. It's an unseemly profession in many ways, not the least of which is the manner in which we gather news. We pick at scabs just forming over wounds recently inflicted, thereby causing new pain for the inflictee and new shame for the inflictor. We even use confidential sources, but generally in ongoing governmental or political cases, when we need information that's reliable but otherwise unavailable."

"Meaning you don't think Coyne was a source for her?"

"Meaning she didn't discuss it with me, though I assume she must have with someone. Meaning also that in reporting, sources in the criminal world run a very distant third to sources in government and politics."

"Some reason she wouldn't have discussed Coyne with you?"

A different look came into Peete's eyes, a gleam that pushed back the glaze for an instant. "Perceptive, quite perceptive. I fear I was to Jane what is politely known in the trade as a police buff."

"A reporter who likes cops?"

"No, a reporter who is fascinated by the police function. There are many officers I like and some I dislike, but the idea, the *con*cept of the law enforcement function is one which never ceases to intrigue me."

"So, if Jane thought that Coyne might be in danger from the cops, she never would have come to you to talk about it."

"Just so. Though if she had, I could have assured her that the police need not stoop to homicide to seal the lips of a felon as vulnerable as the soiled Mr. Coyne."

I already knew that argument. "I understand that the cop supposedly on the take from Coyne's employer is tied into the hierarchy down here?"

"Nasharbor is technically a city in the geopolitical sense, given its population and form of municipal government. But in many ways it is a very small town, and nepotism in city services is one such way."

"Assuming I understand the principle, care to provide the relevant illustration?"

"Careful, Sancho. You converse with me long enough, you'll begin to affect my prolix patterns of speech." He sucked down another two shots of booze. "Now, where were . . . yes, yes the social register of our constabulary. First, the current chief is a figurehead, the first Porto to hold that place, thanks to some clever maneuvering a few years back by our state representative."

"What kind of maneuvering?"

"I'm not a lawyer by training, but I understand the statutory framework to be that one becomes chief through various civil service standards and tests."

"And?"

"And our current chief, bless him, would have trouble signing his name in a legible fashion. However, the aforementioned state rep had the crucial vote in committee on somebody's pet pork barrel as the legislative session clock approached midnight, and the trade was our vote on the pork barrel in exchange for a special statute exempting the position of chief of Nasharbor from any civil service requirements."

"New one on me."

"Yes. Rather shakes one's faith in the democratic process, doesn't it? In any case, however, the current chief is nearing retirement, with two potential successors vying in the wings."

"Namely?"

"A second Porto, Joseph Hogueira, the captain of uniforms here. And Cornelius, or Neil, Hagan, the captain of detectives."

"Jane mentioned Hagan."

"As well she might. Hagan took personal charge of Coyne's death. And the cop allegedly, and I stress allegedly, on the take from Gotbaum, Coyne's nefarious employer, was one Mark Schonstein, son of Hagan's former partner when Hagan was in uniform."

"And Jane figured that Hagan would bury a murder as a favor to an old partner's kid?"

"Well, it does go a bit deeper than that."

"How do you mean?"

As he spoke, Peete regarded the remaining four fingers of vodka with renewed respect. "There was an incident, oh perhaps fifteen years ago. Way before my time, so I've heard only the retellings. But basically, Hagan and Schonsy—that's what everyone called the elder Schonstein, Schonsy—Hagan and Schonsy are on patrol when they pick up a local punk on some kind of charge. Perhaps 'Failure to Give a Good Account of Himself.' That was a wonderful catchall when I worked in New Jersey. Anyway, there's a row in or near the cruiser, and when they get to the hospital, Schonsy is covered with his own blood, and the kid is dead of a broken neck."

"Schonsy killed the kid in a struggle?"

Peete shook his head. "The way the story goes, the

kid attacked Schonsy, and Hagan hit the kid to get him off his partner, but the impact was at just the wrong angle, causing the fatal spinal injury."

Maybe Jane wasn't entirely off the track after all. "You see it that way?"

"I've covered the police in ten different cities over a checkered thirty years. I've yet to see a cop not back up his partner."

"You also think Hagan buried Coyne's death as a payback?"

"Please, good sir. Be serious. After all this time, Hagan is going to risk hurling his promotion to chief into the toilet to do another favor for an old partner whose life he already saved once?"

"If that's the way it happened, no."

Peete started waving toward the bartender, and I got up to leave before he had another. Bottle, not drink, that is.

FIVE

Walking past the receptionist, I said, "Arbuckle is expecting me."

Down the corridor and back inside the city room, I was struck again by the din. If Jane Rust did have a confidential source, Coyne or anybody else, I couldn't see her trying to talk by telephone over the noise in the air.

Holding a sheaf of papers and a red Flair pen, Arbuckle came out a door, mumbling to himself. Through the opening and to his rear, I could see a conference table and six or eight people rising around it. I was moving toward Arbuckle when she appeared behind him and looked at me full flush.

"Beth!" The word was out of my mouth before I could think better of it.

The woman smiled. The hair and the eyes were

identical, but the neck was too long, the teeth too big. . . .

She said, "Close but no cigar, friend. It's Liz, Liz Rendall. Do I know you?"

"No. You just remind me of someone. Sorry."

Arbuckle said, "Liz, moonstruck here is the private eye from Boston. He gets today, no more, then he's gone. Got it?"

Instead of acknowledging him, Rendall said to me, "Had lunch yet?"

"No."

"Come on." She put the papers she was carrying on a desk near Peete's and threw a sweater around her shoulders, shawl-style.

"Don't ask me why they call it the Village Inn, since there's no place for sleeping over and Nasharbor hasn't been a village since before the Civil War, but the menu will remind you of Mom's own cooking."

The place had plate-glass windows, Formica tables, and vinyl booths. There was a soda fountain on one side and Andy Williams coming over the tinny stereo system. I ordered Today's Special: a cup of soup, grilled tomato and cheese sandwich, and an iced tea. I decided not to commit to the Indian pudding just yet. Aside from Liz Rendall and me, the only person in the place under sixty was our waitress.

"Why so many senior citizens?"

Rendall sipped her water. "Because the owner here offers them a special two o'clock to five o'clock discount. And because fifty cents off means they can ride the transit bus down and back and have a meal out for the price of the meal alone." She looked around the restaurant. "A lot of these people are close to the line. I like to frequent a place that gives them a break." She took another sip and asked her question through the glass. "So who do I remind you of?"

I thought about passing it off, but instead said, "My wife."

She glanced down at my hands. "A guy like you should wear a ring."

"My wife died."

She set down the glass. "Oh. Oh, I'm sorry."

"I am, too. For leading you into it like that. It wasn't intentional."

Rendall looked at me a little more closely. "No. No, I don't think it was. Intentional, I mean. I can see why Jane must have trusted you."

"Did she trust you?"

"About her source, you mean?"

"Yes."

"Not exactly. She told me about having one, sort of seeking my advice about what to do. But she didn't tell me his name until after . . . after he was dead."

"Jane implied to me that she'd revealed Coyne to more than one person. If you weren't one of them, who might have been?"

She grew thoughtful. "Hard to say. You just met Jane that once?"

"Yes."

"I don't know how she struck you, but I interviewed her when she applied here. On first impression she seemed serious, diligent, willing to dredge up the mundane stuff that keeps a paper from printing mistakes."

"What about on second impression?"

"Well, after you got to know her, or better, tried to get to know her, you realized that she created her own little world in which she was the center. Kind of a messiah complex."

"That she'd be the one to save the situation?"

"Right. And anybody who tried to rein her became part of the conspiracy."

"Do you think there was some conspiracy regarding Coyne's death?"

Rendall laughed. "Have you met Neil Hagan yet?"

"No. Given Arbuckle's time limit on me, I thought I'd start at the paper."

"Well, when the present chief retires, one of two captains will replace him. Hagan is new school, smart, professional, the kind of man who as chief will move this city into the twenty-first century."

"And Hogueira?"

She nodded. "Done some homework, I see."

"Some."

"Extending the metaphor, Hogueira leads us from 1890 to 1892."

"Hagan's conscientious?"

"And then some. I don't know how Jane could have thought he'd be involved in sweeping Coyne's death under the rug."

"Maybe because of Schonsy, Junior being both Coyne's target and the son of Hagan's old partner?"

"Your homework consists of talking with Mal Peete, right?"

"Mainly."

"Peete's a drunk, Mr. Cuddy. And about as screwed up in his perceptions of reality as Jane was."

"How're you at perceiving reality?"

"I may not be the best there is, but I'm probably the best you've got. Shoot."

"A couple of people have mentioned some real estate developer named Dykestra."

"Little Richard."

"Who?"

"That's what I call him. Richie Dykestra comes in at maybe five-five. Petty, I know, but he inspires that kind of thinking about him."

"If Coyne's death happened as reported, but Jane's death wasn't an accident or suicide, could Dykestra have been involved?"

"Boy." She paused, chewing. "He's into some shady stuff. And I'm not sure which way Bruce Fetch goes on that one."

"Who's Fetch?"

"Jane didn't . . . no, of course she wouldn't. Bruce and Jane were dating."

"Serious?"

"He was. And three months ago, I would have said she was, too. But lately, I think the fire was mainly at his end."

"Fetch works for Dykestra?"

"You could say that."

"Seems a little out of character, Jane dating a guy who works for the target she's investigating."

"You haven't quite got it. The local redevelopment authority floated Dykestra through this condo project he's doing."

"Dykestra has a debt problem?"

"Are you kidding? His file at the bank is probably thicker than Argentina's."

"And the Nasharbor Redevelopment Authority bailed him out?"

"That's right. And guess who's executive director of the honorable NRA?"

"Fetch."

"Gold star."

"You pick that up from Arbuckle?"

"What?"

"That expression, gold star."

Rendall smiled. "He picked it up from me. Know why he suggested you talk to me?"

"Because he wanted me off his back."

"Partly. But he's also afraid of me, and therefore he'd love to see me step in the shit some time soon."

"Why is he afraid of you?"

"Because he thinks I'm after his job."

"Are you?"

"You bet. With the right managing editor, that little printing press could be a real force in this town, not a dull, safe tabloid that keeps everybody looking rosy to the readers."

"Now you sound like Jane Rust."

"With one major difference. I know what I want and how to get it. Speaking of which, how about dinner at my place?"

She threw me off a little. "I . . . I'm seeing somebody in Boston now."

"Exclusively?"

"Uh-huh."

If Rendall was disappointed, she didn't show it. "Does that mean you're driving back tonight?"

"No, I plan to stay down here for a while."

"Why?"

"Jane paid me for three days' worth. Still two to go."

"And if two more's not enough?"

"This is my slow season, anyway."

Rendall put her fork on the table. "In that case, at least let me help you."

"How?"

"You're the investigator. You tell me."

"What do you think the chances are of Arbuckle letting me see the paper's morgue?"

"Slim and none. Why?"

"I'd like to read some of Jane's stories, especially on Coyne and the development angle. I also want to read about some trouble Hagan had fifteen years ago."

She squinted. "What trouble?"

I told her what Peete told me.

Rendall thought about it. "I can look all that up in the morgue, which by the way the *Beacon* calls its 'library.' The recent stuff on Coyne and Dykestra I can Xerox, but the old stuff would be on the micro. It can't literally be copied, but I'll take some notes for you."

"I'd appreciate it. Witnesses, other information, follow-ups."

"Anything else?"

"Maybe. Jane said she wrote a story on the police corruption angle, but it never got published."

"I remember that from story conference. Arbuckle got all bent out of shape and basically impounded Jane's draft of it."

"Would Jane have any preliminary notes?"

"Don't know. I'll check her desk at the *Beacon.*"

I finished my iced tea. "Do you know who's taking care of the funeral arrangements?"

"For Jane?"

"Right."

She inhaled deeply. "I guess I am. I'm executor—or executrix, I think they call it—under her will."

"You are?"

"Just after Jane got here, somebody in her college class died in an auto accident. Jane insisted on having a will, and she felt she knew me better than anyone else in town."

"Any relatives?"

"An aunt in Kansas. I called her this morning. She'll come in when I can give her the details."

"I don't envy you."

Rendall nodded. "Where are you going to stay?"

"I don't know. Any suggestions?"

"There's only one non-fleabag. The Crestview, just southeast of downtown on Crestview Road. Get the picture?"

"Restaurants?"

"After one night here, you'll find they're terrible. That's where I'll come in."

"I'm sorry?"

"My place for dinner, remember?" She motioned to our waitress for the check.

SIX

After leaving Liz Rendall, I thought I should get to the Crestview before it filled up. I needn't have rushed.

Granted, it was at the crest of the road, and it did have a view of the harbor, if you could sort of block out the auto salvage yard and Sal's Sub Shoppe across the street and downslope toward the water. The motel itself was one long string of gray units with green doors and window trimmings, lying on a diverging parallel from the road itself, as though the architect's square was a bit off. The signs in front of the elliptical drive read, respectively: CRESTVIEW MOTEL, COLOR TV, WATER BEDS, NO CREDIT CARDS ACCEPTED, and VACANCY, apparently without any space allocated for a NO to accompany the last message. The signs looked as though they were commissioned about ten years apart from painters who didn't agree on the proper formation of most letters of the alphabet.

Each parking space was marked in faded yellow to correspond with its unit number. Counting cars, it appeared three of the roughly twenty rooms were occupied. I pulled into the unmarked area next to an awning that said OFFICE.

As I pushed in the door, a man looked up from the book he was reading behind the counter. He was in his fifties, wearing his hair in the still short but slightly unkempt look service lifers often assume once they muster out. His ears were large, his eyes sharp and not particularly friendly. He also had the most outlandish Fu Manchu mustache I'd seen this side of 1972.

"Help you?"

"Yes, I'd like a room for a couple of days."

"Be twenty-six dollars per night, plus tax."

"You're kidding."

"About what?"

"The rate."

Fu scowled. "You're government employee, it's 10 percent off, except for current, active-duty military, then it's 20 percent off. But you don't look active to me, and Reserve or National Guard don't cut it here."

"I didn't mean it seemed too high. I meant it seemed awfully reasonable."

"Wait'll you see the room."

He slapped a registration card in front of me, followed by a Bic pen. Writing, I said, "I didn't see a sign out front for telephones."

"Why do you suppose that might be?"

"I'm going to be some inconvenienced by not being able to make and receive calls."

"You'll be more inconvenienced by having to drive twelve miles inland to get a phone in your room."

I picked up a dusty business card from the front of a

plastic holder on the counter. The ones behind it were a little whiter.

"This still the number here?"

"Yeah, but I don't take no messages. I'm not a goddam switchboard operator, you know."

"I'll bet you've never been in Public Relations, either."

"I was a master sergeant. Know what that is?"

"It's been a while, but I remember." I extended my hand. "John Cuddy."

He ignored my offer. "I'm Jones. You won't be here long enough to need my first name." He scanned the registration card. "That'll be cash in advance."

I gave him three twenties. "If I'm going to be staying a third night, I'll notify the concierge."

Jones fished a key off a rack somewhere under his side of the counter, making a jingling noise. "Unit 18. The Honeymoon Suite."

"Honeymoon Suite?"

"Yeah. You look like the kinda prevert would get off being in a water bed by himself."

I closed the door of Unit 18 behind me. In addition to containing the promised liquid mattress and color TV, it wore a cake-icing shade of pink on every surface that would take paint. I hung up the sports jacket and khaki slacks on the open-air closet pole next to the bathroom and put my clean shirts, underwear, and jogging gear into the bureau. Brushing my teeth under a flickering light, I tried to decide whether the damage to the tiles in the tub behind me came from destructive children or industrious insects.

I had Jane Rust's address from the check she had given me. Stubborn pride kept me from running it down with Jones, but the gas jockey on the next corner sent me roughly in the right direction.

The street number matched a modest, free-standing two-family on a postage stamp lot. The solitary tree and low bushes looked scraggly and parched.

Leaving the Prelude at the curb, I walked up the cracked cement path to the steps of the front porch. Up close, the wood was warping, the walls peeling. I climbed the steps to the house door. There were two buttons, one with "Rust" and the other "O'Day." Pressing Jane's, I heard an irregular buzzing sound, like a giant bee with laryngitis. Getting no response, I leaned into "O'Day."

From an upstairs window, an elderly woman's voice yelled, "Who is it? Come out so I can see you."

I moved from under the overhang of the porch roof and looked upward. A woman was framed by a light behind her.

"Who are you?"

"My name's John Cuddy. I'd like to speak with you about Jane Rust."

"Jane's dead."

"I know. I'm investigating her death."

"Wondered when you folks would get back around to me. Hold on. These days, takes me a while to get downstairs."

The second-story sitting room was fussy. Too many tables with little evident purpose, and crocheted doilies on every possible plane, flat or curved. Mrs. O'Day sat in a rocker, wattles under her chin and both hands around her cane, tapping its rubber tip on the old carpeting.

"Private investigator, huh?"

"That's right."

"Wasn't aware she had any family to hire someone like you."

"Jane herself hired me."

"Now that she's dead, how come you're still working for her?"

"She paid me for three days' worth. It seems to me she has that coming."

Mrs. O'Day watched me for a moment through Coke-bottle glasses. "Are you an honest man or just a very clever one?"

"I don't follow you."

"Are you honestly interested in Jane and honoring your contract with her, or are you just using that old-fashioned notion to get on the good side of an old lady you need to pump?"

I laughed.

She said, "Well, leastways you laugh honest."

"Mrs. O'Day, Jane asked me to look into something. Then she turns up dead that night, supposedly a suicide. That just doesn't ring true to me."

"Don't know much about suicide. Against the Church's preaching, which makes it kind of hard to understand it. But I can tell you this, she was a mighty troubled young woman."

"Can you tell me what happened last night?"

"Best I can. I was home here, up pretty late planning."

"Planning?"

"Budget planning. I get $473.50 a month social security as sole survivor of the husband, God rest his soul. I never did work outside, so I don't have any account of my own. Rent from downstairs covers the house costs and all, but still got to computate in

53

advance where all of it should go. Today was Store Day."

"Store Day?"

"Yes. The Church, Lord bless it, has a volunteer van, comes to pick up those like me what can't get out on our own. Takes us around to the grocery, the drugstore, laundry, that kind of thing. Regular schedule. Feel mighty sorry for the others."

"What others?"

"Those outside the Church. They're the ones people like you never see, because they ride the buses from ten to two when you're in working. That's the only time the buses aren't so crowded you can get a seat. When's the last time you ever saw a man or child stand so an older person could sit down? Then there's the hoodlums, too. Leastways most of them are still in school of some kind, probably reform school, till two o'clock, so your purses and wallets are safe from them if you're back in and locked up by two. Your generation thinks it's all set, you wait till you get older, sonny. Back in thirty-three, when my daddy started paying into social security, there were sixteen workers for every retired person. Read that in *Reader's Digest,* I did. Sixteen to one. Now there's only about three and a half to one, and by the time you're into your sixties, never mind seventies or eighties, there's only going to be maybe one and a half workers for every retired person. I thank the Lord every night he won't be keeping me down here so long to see that day come, I'll tell you."

"About last night, you were up late?"

"Planning."

"Planning. Did you see or hear anything unusual?"

"See? Not rightly. I've got bad eyesight, need the

two different kind of glasses to see straight, but never could stand having them on those neck strings, you know? So I'm forever putting the distance ones down when I put the close-up ones on, then forgetting where they are."

"Well then, was there something you didn't see but heard?"

"Heard a lot of things. Nothing wrong with the hearing, leastways not yet. Heard Jane coming in all the time. That's the reason I gave the tenant the downstairs floor to start with. I didn't have any use for the backyard myself, and I figured with me on the second floor, I wouldn't be disturbed so much by the coming and going. But this time of year, I keep the windows open, which means I can hear the car doors or the damned, pardon my French, motorcycles or feel the downstairs door close. 'Course, that's more vibration than sound, I guess."

This was going to take a while. "Did you hear somebody arrive last night?"

"Well, yes, of course I did. Heard Jane first. She usually got home from work by six. Ofttimes she'd go out later. Jane was renting from me for nigh unto two years, her car door made a certain noise account of she had something loose there in the door panel or something, rattled every time after the sound of the door closing itself. Think she'd have that fixed, drive you crazy after a while, but she never did."

"You heard somebody else, too?"

"Sure did. Jane seemed to be home to stay last night. Heard her drive in, car door, and downstairs. She'd been in the dumps lately, don't know why, just real troubled, like I said. Well, I hear her come in, put on her victrola. Didn't play it loud or anything, real considerate girl that way. Then I heard another car come up. Somebody got out, come up to the door and knocked, then Jane let them in."

"Them?"

"Him or her. Couldn't tell. They must've cut across the lawn or was wearing sneakers or something, cause I didn't hear any clicks like from the women's shoes or taps like from the men's. Jane knew whoever it was, though."

"How do you know that?"

"Jane knows somebody, she tells them . . . sorry, told them not to ring the bell. Needs fixing and can wake me out of a sound sleep, so she'd warn them not to use it. Considerate that way, like I said."

"No idea otherwise who the person was?"

"No. There were a lot of them, though."

"A lot of them?"

"That didn't use the doorbell. Jane got more than her share."

"Her share of what?"

Mrs. O'Day's eyes seemed to move independently behind the lenses as she leaned forward in the rocker. "Of what? Of sex, what the hell do you think, pardon my French again."

"Did you . . . were you under the impression that it was more than one man?"

"Was I . . . sonny, all I know is I heard a lot of different doors slam out in that driveway, if you get my drift. The Church says we're not supposed to sit in judgment of each other, but even without the suicide, I doubt she got to spend much time before Saint Peter last night."

"How long did this person stay?"

"Hours. Didn't really pay attention to when, I was focusing on my planning here. But they must have been going at it pretty good, because her phone rang four or five times for five rings without her answering it."

"Was that typical?"

"Typical of her going at it, you mean?"

"Typical for her not to answer her phone when she had a man, not a woman visiting."

"Sonny, I don't for one moment believe Jane was that way."

"I didn't mean to imply anything, Mrs. O'Day. I just . . . look, was Jane's failure to answer her phone something she'd do only when she had a male visitor?"

"That I don't know. Like I said, I didn't try to spy on the woman."

"Right. So you don't know when her visitor left."

"No, I don't. Wasn't too long before another one came by, though."

"Another?"

"Right. After the first one left. Another car door, different sound to the motor and the door both."

"Different how?"

"Motor sounded bigger, door more solid. Don't know much more about cars than how they sound. Never got my driver's license. The husband was always after me about that, said I'd regret it some day. But I ask you, how can I regret never learning to drive when I'd be a menace out on the roads with this eyesight? I mean, if I can't keep track of my distance specs in this house, how would I ever remember them each time before I cranked up a car?"

"You've got a point there. Did you hear anything about this second person?"

"No. Except Jane must have been expecting this one."

"Why do you say that?"

"Because this one didn't even knock. Door down-stairs just opened and closed."

"How long did this one stay?"

"Minute, maybe. Then out, banging the door shut and off into the car and tearing up the street to beat the band."

"And no idea whether this second one was a man or woman?"

"Nope."

I thought about it.

Mrs. O'Day said, "I found her, you know."

"You did?"

"Yes. It was the victrola. Like I said, usually she was real good about playing it low, but I was finished with my planning, and I wanted to get four hours of sleep before Store Day. You know, so I'd have plenty of energy. Funny, four hours is enough now, even when I let the planning slide till the night before and I have to stay up most of the night to plan when I had all the week before to do it. Of course, you never know for sure what you really need till just before you go out to buy, and it'd be crazy for me to just stock up at the prices they're getting these days, although when did you ever know the prices on anything to go *down?*"

"Never. You mean her stereo was still on when you tried to go to bed?"

"That's what I said. It was, oh, two-thirty maybe? I tossed and turned for a while, but it was no good, I could still make out the words the radio announcer was saying. If it was just music, I might have been able to ignore it, but you know how it is when somebody's talking, you sort of strain to make sense of the sentences even if you're hearing only a few words from each."

"What did you do then?"

"I went to the telephone to call her. It'd happened before, she'd fall asleep with the radio on and then let it play. So I called her, but I could hear the phone ringing, like I said before, and she wasn't answering. So I went down the back stairs to the kitchen and knocked and called out her name, but she didn't answer that either, so I walked through the kitchen and—"

"Wait a minute. The lights were all on?"

"Well, not *all* on. I mean, Jane did have some respect for the electric, and it never seemed to me to make sense to have the company come in and do separate meters. That's always a waste so long as you don't have some sloth down there, doesn't know how to turn off a lamp."

"But some lights were on?"

"Yes, and then I moved through into the living room and she was on the couch. Lying on it, dead."

"You were sure she was gone?"

"You grew up when I did, sonny, you learned what to look for. And smell for, more's the pity. I remember clearly my mother herding my brother and me in to see Gramp on his deathbed. That's where the expression comes from, you know. In the old days, people actually died in their beds, even when they knew it was coming. They didn't go to some hospital, lying on some stranger's sheets and being felt all over by some stranger's hands. No sir, you sent for the doctor once, and if he said, 'That's it,' you didn't waste anybody's money or the dying person's dignity on some hospital. You let them stay right where they were, in their own house, in the bosom of their family. They could die where they lived, not behind some canvas screen in a cold room. The husband passed on in the hospital, then got dumped into a green bag and wheeled onto an elevator, God rest his soul."

"So you knew Jane was dead?"

"Aren't you listening to me anymore? You watch enough people die, you know what dead is."

"What did you do then?"

"Well, I looked around. But all I saw was some cocoa in a mug long gone cold. So I said a prayer for her right there, though I knew she was damned for taking her own life. I thought I ought to, being I knew her and I didn't see any family of hers likely to arrive before they took the body away."

"There was no note?"

"Note? Well, none that I saw, but I couldn't have read it of course, even if there was one. Had on the distance specs, not the close-ups. I try to go downstairs wearing the reading glasses, and it's me what they'd be finding stiff at the bottom of the steps."

"Mrs. O'Day, did you tell the police all this?"

"As much as they'd hear. They didn't seem to have quite the patience you do."

"Well," I said, "I appreciate all the time you've given me."

"My pleasure. Good to talk with a sensible young man for a change. Don't you want to see her place before you go?"

"The police didn't seal it off?"

"My goodness, no. It was just a suicide."

"In that case, I will, thank you."

"Just don't break anything. I'm not worried about a man like you stealing, but I'd be embarrassed if you broke something."

"A woman at the newspaper is arranging Jane's funeral. I'll call you when I know the details."

"Don't trouble yourself. Funerals depress me. Besides, she was a suicide, remember? The Church wouldn't like for me to be going to one of them."

Except for the narrower sitting room to accommodate the first-floor expanse of staircase outside her door, Rust's apartment was the twin of Mrs. O'Day's. The bedroom contained a pine four-poster with a bedspread that looked like an heirloom. The dressers matched the bed. On top of the lower dresser was a nearly empty jewelry box, some change in a large seashell, and framed, stand-up photos. The first shot was a shorter-haired Jane with a longer-haired Liz Rendall, both in swimsuits. Each had an arm draped around the other's shoulder, Jane looking sheepish and Liz brash.

The second showed an older woman and a much younger Jane, probably in her early teens. They stood at the corner of a house with a flat meadow background that disappeared only at the horizon.

The third photo caught a current Jane handing a drink to a skinny, hippie-like guy sitting on what appeared to be her living room couch. Coyne, maybe?

I plodded around the apartment enough to tell that no forensic team had been there. Nothing apparently was missing except Rust's body. If my client had been killed as part of a "police conspiracy," someone should have tossed the rooms, searching for whatever evidence Jane might have had on the conspiracy. A forensic investigation of a suspicious death would have provided the perfect cover for that kind of search. It didn't seem anyone had bothered, though it's hard to spot a slow, careful search if the place isn't your own to start with.

I skimmed through what files I could find in a box in her closet. They all seemed to be just copies of stories from her previous jobs. Nothing about Coyne or Dykestra.

I closed Rust's door to the front hallway and the outside door to the house, both locks snicking securely behind me. Walking to the Prelude, I looked back at the two-family. An unremarkable place to die.

As I approached the motel, Sal's Sub Shoppe still had its lights on. I got an Italian with everything on it and directions to the nearest package store, Sal warning me that only the bars in town stayed open past ten.

At Nasharbor Liquors, I bought a cold six-pack of Molson Golden ale just as the clerk was cashing out. I tried Nancy from the pay phone outside. No answer.

The odor of oils from the sandwich filled the car on the way back to the Crestview. Loading up on carbohydrates, I watched TV for an hour before surfing to sleep in the Honeymoon Suite.

SEVEN

◆

The Nasharbor police headquarters was on Main Street next to city hall. The department occupied a massive Gothic building with miniature gargoyles on the corners and a modern, masonry block annex. I went through the double doors atop the old steps and walked up to the desk sergeant's Plexiglas enclosure.

The sergeant was olive-skinned with black wavy hair. "What can I do for you?"

"I'd like to speak with Captain Hagan."

"Captain's a busy man. What about?"

"The death of Jane Rust. My name's John Cuddy." I opened my ID under the small slit on the counter.

"Private, huh? Insurance?"

"I'd like to talk with him about it."

"Probably be a while before I can call him."

A bench was pushed against the wall. "I'll time you from over there."

The sergeant shuffled a few forms to save face, then dialed an internal extension.

Hagan folded my ID and leaned back across his desk, careful not to knock over the triptych portraits of wife and assorted kids on the corner. Mounted commendations crawled up the wall behind him. He'd stood and shook hands when I'd come in the room. A little shorter and a little huskier than I am, maybe forty-two or forty-three, with auburn hair in a Madison Avenue cut and a herringbone jacket with elbow patches. Clean-shaven, he looked like the sort who slapped Aqua Velva onto his cheeks in the morning mirror.

Hagan said, "Anybody on Boston I can call about you?"

"Try Robert Murphy, lieutenant in Homicide."

"Don't know him. Anybody else?"

"Yeah, but they'd hang up on you."

Hagan sat back, tenting his hands at belt level. "So what's your interest in Jane Rust?"

"She came to see me on Monday afternoon. She didn't strike me as close enough to the edge to kill herself Monday night."

"She goes to a private investigator, she must have had something bothering her."

"Look, Captain, we can dance around a while longer if you'd like, but we both know why she came to see me. She thought your department was involved in the death of Charlie Coyne."

"You ever meet Coyne?"

"No."

"If he graduated high school, they would've captioned his photo 'Most Likely to Die in an Alley.' Which is exactly what happened to him."

"Suspects?"

Hagan snorted a laugh. "No more than a hundred. When Coyne got drunk, he got sentimental, wanted to share things with his brothers on the street. As in homeless and on the street."

"And you figure one of them did him?"

"One of them saw it. Or at least the end of it. Or at least he thinks he saw the end of it."

"What did he see?"

"Biggish bum, hobbling away after stabbing Coyne. The witness says Coyne managed to knife the killer in the leg."

"The big guy show up at a hospital?"

"Not that we can tell. If he tried to patch himself up, he'll lose the leg within a month. If he crawled off somewhere to die, a pair of uniforms will get a call to investigate a godawful smell coming from some abandoned building."

"You seem pretty casual about all this. You have that many homicides down here?"

"You mean murders, no. You mean deaths by unnatural causes, hell yes. The leading killer of the homeless is frostbite. Right behind is guys beaten to death or stabbed in the heat of passion over cigarettes or a couple of returnable empties, net the guy a quarter maybe."

"I wasn't aware that Coyne was homeless."

"Next thing to. He was shacked up with a girl and a kid she claims is his. You saw the place, you wouldn't let your dog run loose in it."

"Mind giving me her name and address?"

Hagan came forward again, all business. "Look, Cuddy, I can see the position you're in. This girl Rust comes to see you, ends up dead that night. You maybe feel a little responsible, or that you owe her something. Fine. I'd feel that way myself if I were in your shoes. That's why I've been so open talking with you about things. But everybody—me, the medical examiner, the statie attached to the DA—everybody has Coyne down as a simple death by stabbing."

"And Jane Rust?"

"Autopsy and lab report came in by hand an hour ago. She swallowed enough sleeping pills to drop an elephant."

"Except she couldn't."

"Swallow them you mean."

"Yes."

"We found a mug and a tablespoon on her kitchen table. One of the latents on each matched her index finger. The girl ground up a handful of the pills like an old-fashioned pharmacist with the mortar and pestle things."

I thought about it. "Seems a hell of a complicated way to take your own life."

"Rust was a complicated girl under a lot of stress, most of it self-inflicted. Besides, maybe she didn't have a razor handy."

"Any note?"

"No."

"Strike you as odd a reporter didn't leave one?"

"No."

"Aside from the paper, was she under any stress you know of?"

Hagan shook his head. "She's dead now. Whether it was intentional or accidental, it was by her own hand. Whatever problems she had won't get helped by me airing them to a guy I met ten minutes ago."

"I talked to her landlady. She says Rust had two visitors the night she died."

"I spoke to Mrs. O'Day. Personally, face to face. Even with her 'distance specs,' she couldn't tell me how many arms I had."

"She told me she heard car doors slam. Two different cars, two different times."

"The house is in a neighborhood, not the sticks, for chrissakes. She keeps her windows open and ears cocked, she'll hear David Letterman swing by, she stays awake late enough."

I tried a different tack. "I understand you and a man named Schonstein were partnered a while ago."

Hagan got his back up a little. "You understand correctly."

"It's Schonstein's son that supposedly was on the take from the porno peddler, right?"

"That's right. And you be real careful to say 'supposedly' or 'allegedly' every time you ask about that around here, because Coyne and Rust were both full of shit about Mark."

"Mark's the son?"

"That's right. He'll never be the cop his father was, but then nobody will. Schonsy was a god around here, buddy. The kind of cop doesn't just keep the order, he makes the order. He trained every cop in this department's any good at all, including me, from the ground up."

"Mind telling me where young Mark was the nights Coyne and Rust died?"

Hagan ground his teeth. "I hope that's your last question, because it's the last one I'm going to answer. Mark was here, in the station, both nights. Doing paperwork in front of six other officers because his partner was home, sick. Now get out."

I thought better of asking if he meant out of his office or out of his town.

I'd just closed the hallway door to Hagan's office when I heard a gruff voice say, "Hey!"

I turned. A monstrous uniformed officer was beckoning to me, so I walked toward him. The plastic name tag read "Manos."

He said, "Captain wants to see you."

"I just saw him."

The officer moved his hand toward a doorway at the end of the corridor. "Other captain."

"My name is Hogueira. You're Mr. John Cuddy, private investigator from Boston."

I shook his hand and we sat down, the uniform staying inside the office but at the door behind me. Hogueira was about five-eight, probably just over the minimum back before sex discrimination suits wreaked havoc with that requirement. Pushing fifty, mainly around the waist of his uniform pants and Sam Brown belt, he had the same black wavy hair as the desk sergeant downstairs, but with little sideburns and less mustache. His eyes were a warm, chocolate brown, like a particularly loyal and affectionate spaniel. Right.

He said, "I'm told you're looking into Ms. Rust's death."

"Indirectly. She hired me on another matter."

He nodded solemnly, sympathetically. "A difficult situation for us all, Mr. Cuddy."

"How's that?"

He spread his hands expansively. "We are a small city, sir. A poor one in many ways, rich only in our helping of each other. The several deaths weigh heavily in such a community."

"I had the impression Charlie Coyne might have been a tad light in the mourner department."

"Mr. Coyne, who I remember well from his exploits as a juvenile, was not the most popular of individuals. Also, his employment environment was not conducive to long life and happiness. It is the circumstances prior to his death that concern me, however."

"The allegations of corruption."

"Yes, the 'allegations.' That is exactly how you should refer to them."

"Thanks, but I've already heard that advice once this morning."

"My peer, Captain Hagan, advises you well."

I decided not to say anything, let him lead me.

"You see, it is good advice because there are many who would poison the community against the police force. There are enough in the minority community who already wish to do so, despite the fact that our present revered chief is himself of Portuguese descent."

"Would that part of the community be reassured by the appointment of a similarly descended successor when the current chief retires?"

A small smile toyed with the corners of Hogueira's mouth. "Many would be so, yes."

"And a provable corruption scandal on the plainclothes side of the hallway might substantially increase that possibility."

"Very likely."

"But it also couldn't look like the uniform side had given things a boost."

"Oh no!" said Hogueira. "That would be unseemly."

"But perhaps some information, civically shared with a concerned individual like myself . . ."

"Perhaps in the form of more good advice."

"I'm always open to good advice."

Hogueira wiggled his rear end deeper into the chair. "There are several quite dangerous places to be avoided in the part of our city called, unfortunately, The Strip. An area of sex and sin which my uniforms patrol, but are discouraged from investigating. One such place is a theater called the Strand which shows unwholesome films. Another is a bar catering to voyeurs called Bun's."

"Let me guess."

"The management would say you were wrong. They would say they drew the title from the nickname of the owner, one Bernard 'Bunny' Gotbaum. But your guess about the quality of entertainment offered there would be distressingly accurate."

"Is there any special reason I should stay away from these two places?"

"Oh yes. The unfortunate Mr. Coyne was employed at the Strand, and he died behind Bun's after drinking heavily there."

"Captain, if Coyne had lived, would the DA have sought an indictment against whoever on the force was allegedly involved in the porno business?"

"You ask a question that a man in my delicate position should not answer. I believe, however, that without Mr. Coyne, no district attorney could possibly present a successful case. The state police investigator in that office, a Trooper Cardwell, might offer the same opinion, if you were to ask him."

"Hagan said that a bum in the alley saw Coyne's killer and that Coyne was living with a woman somewhere around here. Can you help me out with their names?"

"Mr. Cuddy, you should have learned by now that one captain cannot discuss a case assigned to another captain. I trust that you will take my good advice." He glanced over my shoulder. "Officer Manos will be pleased to escort you from the building now."

EIGHT

I drove up the road fifteen miles or so to the district attorney's office. I was lucky: a secretary covering the front desk said Trooper Cardwell was in.

She pointed to his office, a slope-sided garret with another desk in it and the headroom of an attic crawl space. Seated in a low-back, wheeled chair, Cardwell was black and under thirty. He wore a military haircut and bearing, over a short-sleeved dress shirt and yellow tie. After we introduced ourselves, I closed the door behind me.

Cardwell said, "What's on your mind?"

I sat across from him and said, "Charlie Coyne and Jane Rust."

With a toe, he propelled himself around to use the telephone. "References?"

"On me?"

"That's who I'm talking to, isn't it?"

"Try Lieutenant Murphy, Boston Homicide."

Cardwell's eyebrows perked up an inch. "Robert Murphy?"

"That's right."

"You give me his name because he knows you well or because he's black?"

"Both."

Cardwell stifled something, but whether a laugh or a curse, I'm not sure. He'd acquired the knack of stifling.

After dialing and routing through some transfers, he said, "Lieutenant Murphy? Sir, this is Trooper Oliver Cardwell. I'm attached to . . . thank you, sir, I remember that, too. . . . Lieutenant, I've got a private investigator sitting in front of me named Cuddy, first name John, says he . . ." Cardwell grinned. "Nossir, I haven't been vaccinated recently . . . yessir, he looks that way to me, too. . . . You say so, that's good enough for me. . . . Right, right, look forward to it, Lieutenant."

Cardwell replaced the receiver. "Murphy says you're an asshole."

"See?"

"Says I'd be better off throwing you out the window than down the stairs on account of you might hurt the stairs."

"Good old—"

"Says you fuck me up down here, he'll take more than your weapon by the time you check your next mail delivery."

"So he said you could trust me. Can I get on with this?"

Cardwell eased back. "You can get started, anyway."

"I already did. Charlie Coyne and Jane Rust."

"Way you say that, you think they're connected. Doesn't look that way to me."

"I'd like to hear it."

"You talked with Hagan down to Nasharbor yet?"

"Yeah."

"And he didn't tell you much or show you much, so you came up to me."

"That's right."

"You know anything about my position here?"

"I know the state police supplies investigators to the DA's. I know you guys are supposed to run the major crime stuff for the local cops in the smaller towns, but you don't get much involved in Boston. That's about it."

"Right as far as it goes. Problem for us is political."

"That's a surprise."

"Yeah. Everybody starts in uniform on highway patrol. You request investigation, maybe you get assigned to the Bureau of Investigative Services, and maybe, if a DA wants you, you get assigned to a CPAC unit—that's Crime Prevention and Control—in a DA's office."

"I'm with you so far."

"Well, in case you haven't been doing a lot of highway driving lately, there ain't a fuck of a lot of troopers of color on the roads. So when I requested investigation, where you figure I'd be assigned?"

"Someplace there are a lot of people of color, where a black face on a cop might make a real difference in whether the jury gets to hear the witnesses who saw things go down."

Cardwell canted his head, reassessing something. "Instead I'm down here. Know why?"

"Politics."

"Good guess. The DA down here is on the outs with

74

the current administration. That means every time one of his investigators gets good enough, the trooper or corporal gets promoted and finds himself riding a sergeant's desk in a barracks someplace, rearranging patrol patterns instead of looking into homicides and related major action. Guy I replaced seven months ago's doing that, and if I get good enough, same thing'll happen to me, unless I decline the promotion."

"Sounds pretty counterproductive."

"It is. But it helps you appreciate where I stand. And where you stand."

"And where's that again?"

"I stand where allegations of police corruption in local departments that support the DA don't get taken at face value, and you stand somewhere out by Montana unless the Nasharbor force tells me to cooperate with you."

"What if I don't ask to read the paperwork or anything. What if I just want to talk a little about the crime scenes themselves?"

Cardwell used a strong hand to rub on his chin. "Try an easy one first."

"You see Coyne before they took him away?"

"No. Nasharbor covered that. I came on it the next morning."

"Anything about it trouble you?"

Cardwell shook his head. "Coyne was small time. Delivery boy for dirty pictures, videos, and like that." Without changing his neutral tone, Cardwell said, "Mostly kiddie porn. You want to see some of the shit we caught him with?"

"No thanks."

Cardwell dipped his chin to his chest. "Good. Makes me sick to think about it."

"You think the movies got him killed?"

"Doubt it. Most you could make of it is he steps in something, don't know enough to wipe his shoes before walking through the house, somebody decides he don't get to walk no more. And that's if he was hit on purpose. More likely, it's just bum sticks bum."

"You talk to any witnesses?"

"No. One of Hagan's detectives took a statement from a derelict in the alley. Miracle anybody saw or remembered anything. Statement made things sound pretty typical."

"You see Jane Rust?"

"Yeah. Walked through the place with Hagan himself. No sign of forced entry, struggle, even anybody else being there. Cocoa in the mug, some ground up pills in another one, some—"

"Wait a minute. Two mugs, one with cocoa, and one with the pills?"

"Yeah. Like she used the one to drink from and the other to grind them up. You got a problem with that?"

"Rust told me that afternoon she couldn't abide pills. I guess I can't see her being that methodical about them. Seems to me she'd just grind up a couple in a mug, then run the cocoa right in on top. One mug, not two."

"Assuming she was just trying to fall asleep, maybe. But if she's going off the deep end, and I've never seen more evidence of it short of a notarized bye-bye note, maybe she keeps grinding in the one and pouring in the other till she fades out."

Cardwell made sense. I said, "Anything else?"

"You talk with her landlady yet?"

"Yes."

"Then that's all I've got."

I thanked him and rose.

"Hey, Cuddy?"

"Yes?"

"You bring me something on this kiddie porn shit, I'll think about it. Especially if, and I say again, *if,* the cops are in on it. Jane Rust never even tried me. Don't know why, but she never did. You find something that ain't ranting and raving, something tangible I can tie an evidence tag to, you come back and see me. Otherwise, I don't want to know about you. Got it?"

"Got it."

Someone, maybe Murphy, had taught Cardwell how to swim among the sharks. But I had the feeling he was learning how to grow that extra row of teeth all on his own.

The Nasharbor Redevelopment Authority was tucked above a coffee shop on Main Street, about three blocks down from city hall. I left my car in the municipal lot and walked it, passing on the way one Roman Catholic church with high windows of stained glass and two taverns with low windows of neon beer signs.

At the top of the stairs, a pleasant woman of sixty-plus years looked up from her typing. She was working at a machine that hadn't benefited from electricity, much less memory, at the factory.

"Yes?"

"My name's John Cuddy. I'd like to see Bruce Fetch if he's in."

"Just one moment." She got up and knocked at a door already ajar twelve feet away. She said, "Bruce?," then something lower that I couldn't catch. Turning back to me, she said, "Please go on in, Mr. Cuddy."

He was thumbing through a thick binder of blueprints still rolling up at the edges despite their considerable weight. The binder and a computer monitor and keyboard usurped most of his desk. "Have a seat, be right with . . . you. There it is!"

He marked a place with a sheet of paper while I sat across from him. Knowing he'd dated Jane Rust, I guess I expected an accountant-type, with horn-rimmed glasses, white shirt, and thin black tie. The tie was thin and black, alright, but cut from distressed leather. It hung loosely from an L. L. Bean hunting shirt over wide-wale corduroy trousers. He was about five-ten and maybe a hundred forty with socks. His hair was dark brown, pulled back into a stubbly pony tail. He blinked frequently behind wire glasses that I thought had been unobtainable since "Mr. Tambourine Man" was on the charts. The hippie in the photo on Jane Rust's dresser.

Finally looking up at me, he said, "I'm Bruce Fetch, executive director here. What can I do for you?"

"My name's John Cuddy. I'm a private investigator from Boston. Jane Rust hired me."

Fetch's face was long and expressive, the kind you can watch a thought sink into. This particular thought hit ledge right away.

"I don't want to talk about her. Or why she hired you, okay?"

"Can you give me a reason?"

"Yes, but I don't see I have to."

"You don't, but I understood you dated her. I'd think you'd be a little more interested in her death."

He flared. "I am interested! Maybe I just don't see why I should have to talk with you about it."

"The cops think she took sleeping pills. You ever see her with any?"

"No." Fetch took off the glasses to massage his eyes

with the heels of his hands. "No. She couldn't take them, something about swallowing medicine when she was a kid."

"The cops believe she ground the pills up and then took them in some kind of liquid, probably cocoa."

"I . . . she drank cocoa a lot, but I don't see her doing that. I think she'd sooner get a shot."

"From a needle, you mean?"

"Yes, of course from a needle." He toned down. "But I was wrong enough about her as it was. I could be wrong there, too." He got up and walked to the window, sticking his hands into his side pockets. "Look, just what do you want from me?"

"Jane hired me to look into things down here. One of the stories she was working on involved some projects out of this office."

"Project. Singular. The only live one I've got is a condo site down by the waterfront."

"Is that Richard Dykestra's complex?"

"Yes. It's called Harborside. And right now it's the best thing this town's got going for it."

"Why is that?"

Fetch gestured with his hand across the street. "This town could have been dead. Dead and buried. Fall River and New Bedford were bigger, Taunton and North Attleboro were attracting new industry. We didn't have beaches like the Cape, or nice ponds, or even unspoiled meadows. What we had was a waterfront you couldn't breathe next to for three months starting Memorial Day and a welfare list the size of the telephone book."

"And what changed that?"

"Dykestra. He made some money commercially and started buying up parcels here and there privately. Then he lobbied with our state rep and senator and got a sewer project that made the harbor tolerable. He got funding for this office to push things along. I've got ten, maybe twelve projects that'll fly once Harborside makes it."

"When, not if?"

He turned to me. "That's right. A developer can get all the approvals in the world, but it doesn't mean squat if he can't sell the project once it's built. Richie can do that."

"I'm told he's been a little pressed in the cash flow sense."

"You know of anybody trying to accomplish anything who isn't? It's the nature of the beast. You've got to work on a shoestring because you don't know which parcel or project might go. But you can't attract investors without giving the impression that a particular project is the one that will go."

"Sounds like you understand the industry pretty well."

"My job. Part of it, anyway. The part that drives all the other parts." He came back toward me. "If Richie's project makes it, then all the guys, and women, he has working are drawing paychecks, not welfare checks. Harborside will need, the residents of it will need, all sorts of services. Those other ten or twelve projects I mentioned jump off the boards to supplement and eventually expand what Richie does down there."

"All this boom talk put any people off?"

"Off? No. Well, there's always going to be some opposition to any change, even if it is for the better. But we're not exactly raping virgin forests here, you know? You seen our waterfront?"

"Some of it."

"Well, let me tell you. Nobody in his or her right

mind is going to miss the relics Richie will replace. He gets the right support now, the whole character of this area will change. I'm telling you, this city is perched on the edge of greatness."

"What edge was Jane perched on?"

He cooled off and turned away again. "I don't know."

"She told me she was under a lot of pressure at work. Was that all the pressure on her?"

"I told you once, that's none of your business."

"She also told me her personal life was a mess. Was that your business?"

Fetch cried out and came at me, quicker than I would have credited him. He swung an amateurish right at me before I could get all the way up from the chair. I took most of it on my left forearm, and I heard a cracking noise that could only have come from one of his knuckles. He doubled over, holding the right hand in his left palm and grimacing to the point of tears.

"Bruce?" said the older woman behind me.

He squeezed out, "It's alright, Grace. Just leave us alone."

"Are you sure? You look hurt."

"Grace, please. Just shut the door, okay?"

Hearing the door click closed, I sat. "You ought to ice that."

Fetch worked his head up and down. "I'm going to tell you something. Not because it's any of your business, but because I want you hearing it from me first."

His words seemed to be coming a little easier. I said, "Go on."

"I wanted to get married. Jane said she was pregnant."

"I didn't know."

"Neither did I. The baby wasn't mine."

I watched him, then said, "Whose did you think it was?"

He shook his head and gingerly touched around the middle joint of the ring finger on his right hand. "I don't know. I just know I had the mumps in college and the doctor at the infirmary had me give him a specimen. Turned out sterile. Not impotent, just sterile."

Appreciating the distinction, I said, "When I walked in here, you weren't exactly forthcoming. How come now you want me hearing this from you first?"

"Because—shit, this hurts, I think it's broken, that's all I need. Because Richie's deal, the project, is the key to what I've worked for the last two years. I've lost Jane. I don't want to lose what Harborside can mean for this town."

Fetch looked hard at me, seeming to push the hand outside the room for a moment. "I don't want to lose everything."

According to the white pages, Richard Dykestra listed his office under his own name. When I called, a vapid female voice advised me that Mr. Dykestra was "unavailable and not expected in the office today." I told her it was usually one or the other, not both, but she didn't get me, and I couldn't see any sense in leaving a message.

I also looked up Charles Coyne. No luck, but then Hagan had said Coyne's place was a dive.

Looping back toward my car the long way, I stuck my head into the Watering Hole. There were seven customers today. Three even had plates as well as glasses in front of them at two-fifteen. One of the three was Malcolm Peete.

"Mr. Peete, that doesn't look like a very balanced meal to me."

He regarded his vodka and french fries. "Nonsense, my lad. We have here representatives of the two basic food groups, alcohol and cholesterol."

I sat down. "The experts would say you're ruining your health."

"Ah, that's where the Smirnoff performs double duty." He lifted the glass to eye level and rolled it affectionately between his fingers. "Preventive chemotherapy. Requires daily, nay, hourly treatments to be completely effective."

"You sober enough to give me some background information?"

"I'm highly offended. If I'm sober enough to be offended, I'm sober enough to educate the likes of you, good sir."

"Jane's landlady said she had two visitors the night she died. Both came by car. Any candidates come to mind?"

"No. Mrs. O'Day's humble dwelling is far enough from everything to require a car to get there, so I fear I'm your only excludable suspect. I've deemed it inappropriate to drive for some time now."

"Meaning some judge hooked your license?"

"I'll not dignify that with a reply."

"Mrs. O'Day also said Jane had a lot of visitors in general. Male visitors. Aside from Bruce Fetch, was she seeing anyone you know of?"

"No, not really any of my business. Tell me, though, did Mrs. O'Day press upon you her view of the generational conflict ahead?"

"More than I cared to hear."

"Don't be so flip. She's right, you know. The disputes of the sixties between the older and the younger just involved politics and patriotism, comparative trifles. Wait until every worker contributes 40 percent of a weekly salary to social security, and even then the recipients of our federal bounty will be having to choose between heating and eating. That conflagration will make the Vietnam War seem like a crack in the sidewalk."

I let it pass, then said, "What exactly is the corruption situation here? From the police standpoint."

Peete arched protectively over his drink. "There is no 'exact' statement anyone could make. Were you ever a cop?"

"Military."

"Not the same thing. Oh, I'm sure the danger and camaraderie and abilities were quite parallel, perhaps even greater. But you were dealing for the most part with other military. You weren't being paid yearly a tenth of what the bad guys collect monthly. That's the problem, basically. The good cops, and most of them start out that way, the good cops arrest truly bad people and then see them released before they've wiped the fingerprint ink from their hands. Later, even the case you can make slips away because a judge can't see jailing a 'victimless' gambling kingpin when the cell blocks couldn't accommodate another violent offender with a shoehorn. So you get your meat eaters and your grass eaters."

"Translation?"

"I first heard the terms when I was in New York. Knapp Commission, the Serpico matter and all. A meat eater is a cop who asks for a bribe, another license granter the bad guy has to pay on the front end. A grass eater is a cop who basically becomes the bad guy's business partner for a piece of the take, on the back end."

"Don't most departments rotate their personnel every couple of years to minimize that?"

"Yes, and it does, but at the cost of reassigning your most experienced cops in a given area, geographic or specialty, outside the area in which they've become expert."

"So you trade effectiveness off against the fear they've become tainted."

"Quite well put, my lad. However, there is no such fear of that here. At some point before my arrival, the locals divided things up in such a way that rotation was off the negotiating table."

"So the plainclothes guys are the foxes watching the chickens."

"Instead of the uniforms being the foxes watching the chickens, or at least switching off from time to time so that everybody's equally exposed to, and presumably resistant to, temptation."

I said, "What can you tell me about Hagan versus Hogueira?"

"Ah, the Wimbledon of a police buff. Who will succeed the King? In this case, however, I'm afraid it's rather like Ivan Lendl serving to Lou Costello."

"Hagan's a lock?"

"I think so. Thanks to former partner Schonstein."

"The retired cop?"

"Correct. Two of the current city councilors are beholden to the former hero. The paperwork on the drug bust of one's firstborn was conveniently lost; the drunk driving of a second steered miraculously clear of a Breathalyzer test. And not all Schonsy's influence is by way of the fix, either. I nearly cried myself when I covered him doing magic tricks at a party for kids in the local hospital. No, I doubt that Hogueira can convince the others that a second Porto chief in a row constitutes a moral, ethnic, or political imperative."

"Sounds like that special statute you told me about is backfiring."

"Not really. Without the special statute, the current chief would be rattling doorknobs on the midnight shift, Christmas Eve. And with civil service, Hagan would be a shoo-in."

"I don't see that. I've listened to both of them talk. Hagan sounds more like a street cop, Hogueira like an Oxford don."

Peete said, "All form, no substance. Hagan finished college before he started here, then took a master's in police science at Northeastern. Hogueira earned a high school equivalency diploma at night, probably by mail. Resuméwise and testwise, Hagan would trounce him. No contest."

"You a Hagan rooter?"

"No. And yes, I suppose. All cop buffs wonder what would happen if the right man—or woman, I suppose, to be fair as opposed to realistic in this town. In any case, we all wonder what would happen if the right person were put in charge somehow, whether he or she could really make the difference, transform the enforcement of authority into something to be admired rather than abused."

"And you see Hagan as the right man?"

"I see Hogueira as the heir to the old way, the who-you-know way. Don't misunderstand me: the old way is how Hagan will get to sit in the chief's chair. I just think he could be a part of the new way. Or at least I'd like to find out."

"Is Schonsy Junior a part of the new way, too?"

Peete laughed. "Oh no. No, I'm afraid Mark is a pale imitation of his father. I saw Schonsy only at the tail end of his career, but he was the best of the old way, my friend. A Jewish John Wayne who tamed this town for eight hours a day, five days a week. He was the real thing. Mangled his legs coming down the stairs of a burning tenement, carrying a baby out from the flames. Knees at any age are fragile structures, but at sixty, rehabilitation to a patrolman's required agility was out of the question, so he drew a disability."

"Schonsy Senior was only a patrolman when he retired?"

"Yes. And you can just refer to him as Schonsy. I can't imagine anyone calling Mark the son 'Schonsy.' Yes, Schonsy decided early on, I guess, that the street was what made him go, and he never wanted to leave it. I've known men like that before in other departments. It gets into the blood."

"Hagan told me that Mark was in the clear on both Coyne and Jane because he was doing paperwork at the station both nights. Said his partner was sick."

"Sick? Hard to picture Dan Cronan sick. His wife now, that woman would have reason to be sick."

"The partner's married?"

"Correct. And being married to Cronan the Barbarian is not where a woman should spend her springtime."

"Hagan also told me about a bum in the alley who supposedly witnessed part of the assault on Coyne. Any names?"

"Not that I heard. I doubt most of them remember or care to give their real names, anyway. Many are on the run from prior involvements, you know."

"How about Coyne's live-in girlfriend. Name and address?"

"They escape me. I must look into these losses of short-term memory. But the address and probably her name would be in the report on Coyne's death."

"Hagan's not going to let me see it."

"No. I meant the story Jane would have done on it. If the police released it to her."

"Liz Rendall is getting those stories for me."

"That is the second time you have offended me today."

"I don't get you."

"By turning to dear Liz, you imply that I not only am incapable of competent conversation, but also incapable of competent research. Please do me the courtesy of departing."

"Peete, I'm sorry."

"No apologies are necessary because none are acceptable. Please simply leave so that a third transgression, however unintentional, does not nip in the bud what I'd hoped would blossom into a reasonable friendship."

From outside, I saw Peete, catching the bartender's eye and pointing to his nearly empty bottle.

NINE

I called Dykestra again from a drugstore on the way back to the car. His receptionist still couldn't help me. I tapped the plunger and tried a different number.

"Suffolk County District Attorney."

"Nancy Meagher, please."

"Hold on."

Two clicks and two rings. "Nancy Meagher."

"Do they let you receive obscene phone calls at work?"

"Hmmmmmn. Only when the felon involved is beyond the reach of process. Hold on." I could just about hear her saying, "Tell him I'll be with him in a minute." Then, back to me, "How are you?"

"I'm fine. Nasharbor, on the other hand, can use some work."

"Dreary?"

"And then some. You pressed?"

"A little," she said. "How's the case going?"

"It seems that my late client was more than met the eye."

"Meaning you won't be back in Boston for a while?"

"I'm afraid not."

"I'd invite myself down for the weekend, but this rape trial looks like it's going into next week."

"I'm hoping to wrap things up by Friday, anyway."

"Listen, John, I've got to go. Can I call you tomorrow night?"

"My motel doesn't have phones."

"What?"

"It'd take more time than you've got to explain it. I'll try to let you know when I'll be back."

"Good. Take care of yourself, huh?"

"Think about me."

Nancy dropped her voice a notch. "Always."

I drove back to the Crestview, centering the Prelude carefully between the lines in front of Unit 18. As soon as I opened my car door, two men exited the driver and passenger sides of a beige four-door Ford with a whipped-down antenna three spaces away. Approaching me, they couldn't have looked more like cops if shield numbers had been branded on their foreheads.

The first one, younger and balding, flipped open his ID anyway. The second one, older, with a crew cut, was beefy with huge hands and the jacket to a gray suit worn over baggy khaki pants.

The first one said, "Police. Inside."

"You're Mark Schonstein, right?"

The second one said, "The man said inside, pal. Now."

"And that makes you Cronan."

Schonstein said, "You can walk in, or we can carry you."

"It's a nice day. Why don't we just sit on the grass? Kind of like senior seminar in the spring?"

Cronan said, "What's the hardest you ever been hit?"

"Why?"

"Because if I know the hardest was a linebacker, or some guy with a baseball bat, then I know how hard I gotta hit you, make you realize that when we say something, we mean it."

"I remember bumping into a hall monitor at the drinking fountain. Must have been third grade. Wanna see my scar?"

A crusty but familiar voice said, "What the hell's going on here."

Schonstein and Cronan turned to look at Jones. Schonstein said, "Police business. Butt out."

I said, "Mr. Jones, could you call Captain Hagan at the station and ask him if he sent Jan and Dean here to sing to me?"

Cronan said, "Just one more word, pal."

Jones said, "What the hell do they want with you?"

"We haven't gotten around to it yet, but if they had a warrant they would have shown it to me. If you don't give them permission to come into my room and I don't either, we can have their asses if they try something."

Jones said, "Oh, they ain't gonna try anything. Are you, boys?"

Schonstein began to hyperventilate.

Cronan boiled potatoes between his ears. "I don't forget this kind of shit, pal."

"Looks like a nice grassy patch right over there."

They followed me to the one tree throwing any shade and stayed standing while I sat and aligned my back against the trunk. Jones watched us from the doorway to his office, smoothing down the fangs of his mustache.

Schonstein said, "You're playing with fire, Cuddy."

"How about you hear me out, then ask any follow-up questions you've got?"

"Say it."

"Hagan didn't send you guys, and I'm told your dad was a hell of a cop, so I doubt he sent you either. Think this through. If you're mixed up in something like this, even innocently, you're just making it look worse by rousting someone who probably can't lay a glove on you."

Cronan said, "You got a big mouth."

"Look, Cronan, I've heard you were home sick the nights that matter. If that's true, you've got nothing to worry about. If it's not, you do. Either way, banging away at me doesn't help the situation."

Schonstein said, "Coyne was a hustler."

Cronan cut in. "The kinda guy would queer a priest, he got the chance."

Schonstein said, "You think I'm gonna let you try to tie me up with him?"

"I'll tell you what I think. I think it's damn peculiar the way people die down here. Things happened in Boston that happened here, just a whiff of police involvement and they'd be counting the shingles on your roof, just to be sure you didn't have any you couldn't account for."

Cronan said, "You ain't in Boston now, pal."

"That's right. But I was when Jane Rust hired me, and I'll be back there only after I'm finished here."

Schonstein said, "You'll be finished here soon enough, we yank your license."

I shook my head. "First, you haven't got the juice. You can start the process rolling back at the Department of Public Safety, but you can't just reach out and grab it. Second, you're a little shy of grounds. Hagan himself told me the files on both Coyne and Rust were closed. That means there's no ongoing investigation I'm interfering with. Unless you can enlighten me there?"

Schonstein thought it over. "Let's go, Dan."

Cronan said to me, "Maybe sometime I catch you in an alley someplace. No badge, no bullshit. Just you and me. Then we'll find out if your balls are as big as your mouth."

They turned and strode back to their unmarked sedan. Schonstein wheeled out, peeling some rubber in front of Jones.

I raised my voice. "Thanks for backing my play, Mr. Jones."

He said, "First name's Emil. What're you doing for dinner?"

"John, now that's a good name. Strong, but common enough, you don't start folks laughing when they hear it. Ever known anybody named Emil?"

"Not till now."

"Didn't think so. Growing up, other kids gave me hell to pay on it. One squirt, thought he was tough, called me Emily in front of a couple of girls."

"And?"

"And he found two of his teeth right off. Probably swallowed the third one."

I laughed politely and reached for another Killian's

Irish Red ale on the kitchen counter. Jones had bought some barbecued chicken from a local place that did a terrific job on the sauce and the skin. While he heated it up, I drove to the liquor store for a couple of six packs. His dinette set just about filled the floor space between refrigerator and stove.

Emil said, "This Killian's is pretty good stuff. Come out of Boston?"

"No. I think it's part of Coors. Our breweries are trying to make a comeback, but they're kind of boutique operations so far."

"Back in the service, I got a taste for the stronger beers. German, mostly."

"That where you were stationed?"

"Right. Air Defense Artillery. Near transferred to Field Artillery once I found out not many of us were going to Nam."

"You didn't miss much."

Jones said, "Figured you were there."

"That why you stood up against Schonstein and Cronan?"

"Nah. Them two shits, the one's a jerk and the other a bully boy. I just liked the way you didn't let them push you. You don't stand against them every time, there's ten more like them next week, like they multiplied or something."

"Still, you piss them off, they could let you down when you need them."

"Not really, least not in this business. It's not the detectives ever do you any good. The uniforms, they're the ones you gotta keep happy, 'cause they're the ones put it on the line if twelve bikers all of a sudden decide to homestead in one of your units."

I picked up a wing. "You know Schonsy? The father, I mean."

"Yeah. He was a uniform, and a good cop. Tried not to crack any heads less he had to, but the best I ever seen once he got started. More chicken?"

"Please."

Jones carved the second leg off and said, "White meat or dark?"

"Whichever you like less."

"Married?"

"Me?"

"Yeah."

"Not for a while," I said. "Why?"

"You seem to have awful good manners for a husband. Usually the wife wears it out of you."

"You ever married, Emil?"

"Once. Bad idea." He set the platter back on the table. "Didn't really want a wife. Really wanted somebody just to be thinking about me when I wasn't around. No kinda reason for getting hitched."

"I've heard worse."

"Maybe. But my case, it soured me. You know, you give a hundred orders a day to troopers denser than the ammo they're loading, it's kind of hard to break that when you go home to the missus. She wants to get her two words in, and they ain't always 'Yes, dear.'"

"Kids?"

"Nah. Just as well. Had a puppy once when I was little, really got a kick out of watching him grow up. Then once he hit a year or so, I kind of lost interest. Always figured the same would happen with a kid. Plus, the Big Green Machine ain't no place to raise kids right, even if you love the hell out of them."

"How do you mean?"

"Well . . ." Jones put his fork down and took a swig of ale. "The military's a good life for somebody like me. No skills, no college or nothing, enlisted right out of high school. You grow up beginning at age eighteen, but you already had another life. Things get tough, you can look back on it. Kind of, I don't know, draw strength from it or something. You get raised on an army base, though, you lose that. . . . I don't know what you'd call it."

"Perspective?"

"Yeah. Perspective's a good word for it. You lose that, or I guess you don't have it to start with, your whole world's been the army, you don't ever appreciate there's another one out there, maybe's got some good ideas going for it you oughta know about."

"How'd you end up here?"

"Wife's family was from Nasharbor, and we spent some holidays here. They're mostly dead now, but I kind of liked this part of the country. They aren't quite as crazy around here as other places I've been."

"Why the motel business?"

"Saw the Crestview was for sale the last time I was back here burying one of the wife's relatives. She'd bugged out on me by then, but the funeral was a good excuse for an emergency leave. Day before I had to head back, I come out and talked to the owner. He'd been navy, and he was dying, fixing to go into a VA hospital his last couple of months. He gave me the feeling this sort of job would be interesting."

"Was he right, Emil?"

"Depends on whether you find bankruptcy interesting."

"That bad?"

"No, but it depends. Everybody thinks these little places are gold mines, you know? They count the units, let's say it's twenty like I got here, and they do the figures in their heads and come out to twenty rooms times twenty or so bucks which is four hundred a day times seven days is near three thousand a week. That's a hundred fifty thousand a year, and they figure to pay the place off in two, maybe three years, then roll in the gravy."

"But what's your occupancy rate?"

"That's where you gotta start, alright. I think nationwide the average is something like 65 percent per night, but that includes all those resorts run 90, even 95 percent in season. Place like this, no tourists staying reliably for weeks at a time, 25 or 30 percent's more like it. So, right away, your intake's way less than the max."

"And expenses?"

"You wouldn't believe it. Insurance? Off the scale since that singer won the case saying the motel should have kept that guy from attacking her. Then there's air conditioners, mattresses and springs, new TV's, you name it. Every year something major needs replacing. And that's with me doing all the electrical and plumbing and the building inspector doing some winking."

"Think you'll stay with it?"

"Hard to say. The really tough part's you never get a day off. You're here twenty-four hours a day, seven days a week, and boy, that gets tiresome." He crossed his knife and fork on the plate. "I got some cherry vanilla in the freezer, and the Red Sox are going to be on the cable."

"Thanks, but I'm stuffed, and I've still got work to do tonight."

"Work? Where?"

"Couple of places called the Strand and Bun's. Know them?"

Jones winched the Fu Manchu up over his front teeth. "Work, huh?"

TEN

The directions Jones gave me were excellent, but even without them I wouldn't have had any trouble finding The Strip. I joined four other cars cruising it north to south, then made a U-turn and came back south to north. The movie theaters had old-fashioned marquees showing as many bulbs dead or missing as lit. The windows of the strip joints had publicity photographs of women even a feminist would call bimbos, the hairdos dating from the mid-sixties. The bookstores advertised peep shows and prices in hand-printed signs.

The Strand was in the second block, Bun's diagonally across the street in the third. Parking spaces were plentiful, most of the patrons seeming to be pedestrians. I left the Prelude in front of the Strand and approached the ticket window.

A faded, fat woman obliterated all of what must

have been a cocktail stool under and behind her. She looked at me through a streaked and scratched glass window thick enough to be bulletproof. She said, "Three features, seven bucks, no repeats."

"I want to see Mr. Gotbaum."

"Can't help you."

"Can't you call him?"

"Mister, I just sell tickets here. I look like an executive secretary to you?"

"Somebody tried to stick you up, there a buzzer or something you can push?"

She gave me a different kind of look. "I don't want no trouble."

"I'm not trying to give you any. Just call somebody who can get me to Gotbaum."

After thinking it over, she put a hand under the ticket counter, pressed twice, and brought it back. We waited for thirty seconds. Then the blacked-over door to the theater opened and a tall, skinny kid came through it. He had dirty blond hair made to appear dirtier by being slicked back, and his double-breasted, chalk-stripe suit was a size too large for him. As he got closer, I put him nearer to thirty than twenty, but he still looked like his mother had been scared by an early Richard Widmark film.

"This guy giving you trouble, Connie?"

I said, "No trouble. I just want to see Mr. Gotbaum."

"Mr. Gotbaum, he don't see many people."

"It's about Charlie Coyne and Jane Rust."

He smirked. "What, you think you hit a magic button or something?"

"I look like a cop to you?"

He stopped smiling. "You got ID?"

"Yeah." I showed it to him. "But I'm not a cop."

"You're not a cop."

"No."

"Then why the fuck you ask me whether I thought you was or not?"

"I asked you if I looked like a cop. I think I do. I think your customers, probably all five of them, will think so too. Especially if I walk up and down the aisles a few times and stare them in the face a minute or so each. Then maybe I'll stand out here, on the nice public sidewalk by the ticket office, and stare for a minute or so into each face that comes to Connie here. I think maybe I could do that for two or three days, and Mr. Gotbaum will want to talk to me."

He said, "That's pretty good, you know?"

"So, how about we save my time and Mr. Gotbaum's money and see him now. Together."

"You carrying?"

"I'd play it that way."

"You gotta leave it with me."

"Not a chance."

He smirked again. "Even better."

Turning, he walked me to the door, holding it open for me. "My name's Duckie. Duckie Teevens."

Bernard "Bunny" Gotbaum sat like a Buddha in a large judge's chair behind a desk piled high with paperwork. Obese, his sausage-like fingers played with the collar of a long-point sports shirt that bulged at each vertical seam. Wearing a toupee the color of cream soda, overall he gave the impression of a man who hadn't burned twelve calories since kindergarten. The teeth, however, earned him the nickname. The upper two front ones bucked out far enough to open beer cans.

The office carpeting didn't match the walls, and the walls didn't match the furniture. A second man, timid and short, was sitting in a subservient chair reading from what looked like an invoice. From somewhere behind the rear wall, I could hear the projected sounds of a woman faking ecstatic and somewhat extended groans.

Gotbaum glanced up at me and said to Duckie, "The Law?"

Duckie said, "Uh-unh."

"Just a second then." Gotbaum addressed the little guy in the chair. "So you figure we can get *I Only Have Thighs for You* and *The Shape of Things to Come* for the same rental?"

The man said, "Yes, Mr. Gotbaum."

"I like that second title. Any lezzie shots?"

"Just the one, ten minutes before the gang bang."

"Good. That's where they should put all of them. *The Shape of Things to Come*. The guys who come up with these titles. You'd think somebody would have used it already."

Duckie said, "Somebody did, boss."

Gotbaum looked over at him. "They did?"

"Yeah."

"Who? I don't want no product confusion here."

"Old book, boss. Don't worry, none of our customers read it."

"You sure?"

"Positive."

Gotbaum turned again to the guy in the chair. "Okay. That's it then. Call me if the shitheads give you any problems."

The little guy said, "Right, Mr. Gotbaum," and left the room.

Gotbaum sized me up. "So, who are you?"

"My name's John Cuddy. I'm a private investigator looking into Jane Rust's death."

"The tw . . . the one from the newspaper?"

"That's right."

Gotbaum tossed a pencil against the plastic in-box on his desk and said, "Sit down. Tell me what's on your mind."

I sat while Duckie shifted over to the wall, peripherally in sight but well out of reach.

"I'd like to know what you think happened to Charlie Coyne."

Gotbaum said, "What I think happened to him? Dead is what I think happened to him. That it?"

"Not exactly. Coyne worked for you, and Rust said he was a confidential source for her. Now they're both dead, and I'm wondering if you see any connection."

"Connection. Duckie, that's a nice word there, 'connection,' isn't it?"

"Sure is, boss."

I said, "What do you mean?"

Gotbaum said, "You never knew old Charlie, did you?"

"No."

"He was a broad-jumper. World cham-peen."

"Coyne was a track star?"

Duckie said, "The boss means jumping broads."

Gotbaum said, "He saw more ass than a toilet seat, right, Duckie?"

"If cocks was brains, Charlie woulda been Einstein."

"All of which had to do with what?"

Gotbaum said, "Coyne. He looked like a piece of shit. I mean, you saw a photo of the guy, you woulda burned it. Skinny like the Duck here, but no class.

102

Scrungy little beard, one eye green, the other brown, pygmy ears. Nothing. But the broads, I never seen him around one who could keep her hands off him."

"So Coyne was popular. So what?"

"So what? So what if this Rust broad was duking him. Like nightly."

"Maybe twice on Sunday," said Duckie.

"Wait a minute. Coyne and Jane Rust were lovers?"

"Lovers!"

Gotbaum nearly choked on a laugh, Duckie giggled behind me.

Gotbaum said, "I don't know they heard bells ringing or what. Though maybe they was like that. She's the only one I know he was doing he never bragged about it. Even had to drag it out of him. Not like that broad he was living with."

When Duckie didn't add anything, I said, "What's her name?"

Gotbaum said, "His shack-up?"

"Yes."

"I dunno. Duckie, you knew her, right?"

"Don't think so, Boss."

"Oh sure you did. She couldn'ta been more'n a coupla years behind you in school there. Cleary, wasn't it? No. Like that, though. Fearey, right?"

"Maybe," said the Duck.

"Yeah, yeah. Fearey, Gail Fearey. Lives in her folks' house up on Grantland." Gotbaum rested his chins in his hands, drumming fingers on his cheeks. "I'm telling you, pal, Charlie, he would have fucked the crack of dawn, he could get up that early."

"This Coyne used to work for you, right?"

"Kinda. I try to help the unfortunate by offering them jobs."

"What kind of jobs did Coyne do for you?"

"Simple shit. Drive things around for me. Deliver here and there."

"He was busted in a raid next town over, right?"

"Charlie got caught in some kind of net the cops had out that night. I don't know the details."

"I understood he got caught with some movies the Supreme Court says we're not supposed to have."

Gotbaum said, "The Supreme Court. Let me tell you something. I got a lawyer up to Boston, he's a fuckin wiz. He can split hairs a barber couldn't comb. But he tells me, I don't show no kid stuff and no snuff stuff, even fake snuff stuff, and I check ID's, and I can do whatever the fuck I want. Personally, I think it's fuckin crazy. I mean, you know these shows, some of them on TV, they have the little boxes or something for the dummies?"

"You mean close captioning?"

"Yeah, like that. They've got these things so the dummies can find out what the normal people are saying, right? Well, they oughta have little boxes for the guy in the street when the liberals come on the air. They oughta have this little window with a guy telling them that the libbie doing the regular talking is fulla bullshit, because he is. What the hell kind of difference is there between my fuck films and the kiddie stuff, huh? You think fucking or sucking is any different because somebody hits so many years on this earth? The libbies are the ones let me keep open, but they're so fulla shit, I can't stand them!"

Teevens said, "Easy, boss. Take it easy."

"You're right there, Duckie. I shouldn't get so worked up. What else you wanna know?"

"Coyne told Rust that you were paying off some cops to let you stay in business here."

"Paying off. Paying off, huh? You have a blindfold on when you come up here?"

"No."

"Duckie, he keep his eyes closed coming through the lobby and up here?"

"Wide open, boss."

Gotbaum said, "I'm making maybe, *maybe*, my costs here plus 3 percent. You know why?"

"Why?"

"The fuckin Vee-Cee-Are. Videocassette recorder. Used to be, you wanted to see my kinda shit, you have to come to the theaters here. Aw, you'd come maybe with a ski mask on, nobody could recognize you on the way in. I had a Linda Lovelace double feature on once, you'da thought the fuckin terrorists' union was having a convention on my ticket line. A guy wanted privacy, though, he'd have to have a whole fuckin projection system to see films at home. How you gonna hide that from the wife, huh? Or set it up when she's out, she comes in the front door, what do you say, 'Hey, honey, I was just watching the pictures of little Susie's birthday party. What're you doing home so early anyways?'"

Gotbaum really started to fire up. "Now, with the VCR things, any yutz wants to can watch anything. He hears the old lady pulling in the driveway, the cassette's out and back behind the workbench in the basement before she turns the key in the fuckin front door."

"Boss," said Duckie, caution in his voice.

I said to Gotbaum, "So what's your point?"

"My point is, I don't gotta pay off the cops because what I show is legal. And I don't got the money to pay off the cops because I'm barely making a living here with the poor old fucks ain't got the brains or the cash or the house to have a VCR in. Without me, you'd have the poor guys out trying to get laid instead of getting off in here. It's like that football coach used to say."

"What?"

"That football coach. He used to say there are three things can happen when you throw the ball, and two of them are bad. Well, same thing with sex. There are three things can happen: one, you can come; two, she can get pregnant; three, you can get the syph or AIDS or something. And two of them are bad. So, I provide like a public service here. Keep all that from happening to the guys."

"So you don't see the cops killing Coyne at all?"

"The cops, the cops," said Gotbaum. "I'll tell you what I see. I see some guy hearing that maybe Charlie is dropping a dime here and there, get me?"

"Coyne was an informant?"

"Charlie was a little shit, like I told you. When he wasn't working for me, it wouldn't surprise me to find out he was hucking it to the cops on the side."

"And you figure that's what happened to him?"

"No, I figure some bum in the alley did him, like the cops said. Charlie, the way he dressed most of the time, he looked like a bum. But if he was done intentional, I'd bet it was some guy, hears Charlie liked to drop the dime, and says to himself, 'Jeez, maybe Charlie was the guy dropped my brother who's doing eight to ten up in Walpole there the hard way with some jigaboo's putz up his ass.' That's what I figure."

Gotbaum suddenly appeared awfully florid. Teevens said, "Boss, I think you ought to take one."

"Inna minute. You got any other questions there?"

106

"I hear that Coyne was drinking in your bar before he was stabbed."

"That's right. In fact, the Duck was with him that night."

"I was thinking I might go over there and look around. How about Duckie coming with me?"

"Sure. Duckie, go with the gentleman here."

"Not before you take the pill, boss."

"Awright, awright." Gotbaum pulled open the center drawer of the desk and fished around, coming up with a vial of tiny pills. He popped one under his tongue and began taking deep, uniform breaths.

I said, "Nitroglycerin?"

The fat man nodded.

Teevens said, "For his heart."

I said to Gotbaum, "It doesn't bother you that engineers use that stuff to blow away mountains?"

"Naw." He seemed to be completely recovered. "Naw, you just gotta be careful you don't bite down too hard."

They shared a practiced laugh over that one.

"So you like being a private eye?"

I didn't answer until we could trot through a break in the increasing traffic. "It's not bad. You like being an apprentice porno pusher?"

"Could be worse. Least I don't spend my time like most guys, trying to get paid and trying to get laid."

At the door to Bun's, Teevens spoke to the bouncer, an ox with a Duran Duran tee shirt and a bullet-shaped, shaved head. "He's with me."

"Enjoy the show."

I said, "Thanks."

Inside, Bun's opened up into one big room. A raised stage with purple velvet curtains as backdrop occupied the far left corner. Running from the stage and toward the entrance was a bar with a center runway, constructed so that the performers would always be separated from even the bellied-up customers by the bar itself and the moat of bartender space between the bar and the runway. Although no one was on stage, the place was pretty full, ten men for every woman, as best I could see in the dim light.

Duckie said, "Take a seat at the bar. I gotta see a guy here first. Don't order till I get back to you."

I did as he said, telling the bartender who came over promptly that I was waiting for Duckie. The bartender moved away, and I felt long nails squeeze my leg.

I looked up into a tough female face wearing enough eye shadow to fool a male raccoon. The punked-up hair glittered so much that I couldn't tell what color it was.

"I'm Sherry. What's your name?"

"John."

"John. I like that name." She lowered her voice to a whisper. "Wanna fuck my brains out?"

"Thanks, but it sounds like someone already beat me to it."

The smile gave way, but Teevens put his hand tenderly on her shoulder from behind and said, "He's with me, Sher."

Sherry lifted her head defiantly and stalked off.

The bartender came back and Duckie said, "Cal, a round of the boss's stock."

I said, "Just beer for me, thanks. Bottles?"

Cal said, "Bud or Mick."

"Michelob. No glass."

"Right."

Teevens said, "You don't like the hard stuff?"

"Not most of it."

Cal poured Duckie a double shot of Johnnie Walker Black. I made sure I could see the top of the Michelob bottle from the time Cal used a church key on the cap.

After Cal served our drinks, Teevens said, "You're careful. I like that."

"Watching the drinks?"

"Yeah."

"Force of habit. I ask how you figure Coyne died, will I get a straight answer?"

"Not likely."

"Why not?"

Duckie rotated his drink on the bar, leaving artistic whorls of water rings interlinking each other. "Charlie goes into the books the way the cops say, nothing changes. I put in my two cents, maybe I make waves."

"Off the record, what do you think?"

"What, you think I was born yesterday? The fuck does 'off the record' mean to me?"

"Okay. How about what you saw that night."

"The night Charlie got it?"

"Right."

"I didn't see much. Charlie was a real asshole. Bunny told you true there. He used to drink in here a lot, but couldn't hold the shit, even just Bud."

"What's a beer go for when you're not buying it for somebody?"

"Four bucks a bottle. Used to have some on tap for three, but nobody was stupid enough to buy it. Figured it was watered or stale."

"Four bucks. I thought Coyne didn't have two nickels."

"Meaning you don't see him drinking in here a lot."

"That's right."

Teevens gestured toward the empty stage. "Maybe he liked the show."

"A guy who played around as much as you say he did would pay that kind of money to watch strippers on a regular basis?"

"Charlie wasn't no brain trust. Like we told you."

"Gotbaum comped him to the drinks, right?"

Duckie smiled and drank some Scotch. "Yeah, we comped him."

"Why?"

"Bunny, he's a compassionate, generous man."

"No, Duckie."

"Bunny, he grew up with Coyne's old man. That generation down here, religion was no big thing. They were tight with each other, looked after the families. That kind of town, you know?"

"How did you hook up with Gotbaum?"

"Same way. My father and him knew each other. Mine croaked off this stuff," Duckie indicating the liquor on the shelves, "so Bunny give me a job at fifteen. Been with him ever since."

"And you tell him to take his medicine."

Teevens straightened, and for just a second I felt the instinct to fight rise inside him. Then he relaxed and half laughed. "I promised his wife. Before she died."

I let it drop. "You have any idea how Jane Rust got involved with Coyne?"

"Yeah. It was from that raid there. She was after him for some kind of story, and Charlie, he could sense when a broad wanted something he could trade for. Fuck, underneath it all she probably just wanted him to ball her. He sure got caught with his hand in the nookie jar often enough, anyway."

"Jealous husbands?"

"Yeah. Or fathers or boy—" Duckie stopped.

"What's the matter?"

"Shit, man, that was good. That was better than your routine out by Connie there."

"What?"

"Cut the shit. You were getting me to tell you what I thought happened to old Charlie. Indirect."

I downed some beer. "You're a lot brighter than you show, Duckie. Why is that?"

He shrugged. "Don't get you."

"Sure you do. Take your knowing about *The Shape of Things to Come* being a book. H. G. Wells, right?"

"You say so."

" 'Generous,' 'compassionate,' 'indirect' . . ."

"Okay, okay." He took a bigger bite of the booze. "I didn't exactly finish high school, right? But some of the stuff they told us to read was okay. So, I kept after it on my own. Like I'd go over to the community college there, and I'd pick up a book list making out I was some student, and I'd go buy some of the books. All kinds of shit, plays, poetry, whatever. One thing I learned. You ever heard of Maxwell Anderson?"

"Barely. He wrote plays, I think."

"Yeah. There's Sherwood and Maxwell, both Andersons, but I'm talking Maxwell here."

"Go on."

"Well, this guy writes a play called *Barefoot in Athens*. All about how they're gonna kill Socrates. Now the Greek king in the play, he comes across as kind of a clown, okay? So at this one part, Socrates says to the king, 'Hey, you're a lot smarter than you give off. How come?' And the king says, 'You know, when you come on stupid to people, they don't bother you so much. Lets you live okay without them figuring they got to get rid of you. Which gives you time to get rid of them first.' Well, that made a lot of sense to me."

"Be smart, don't look smart?"

"Right, right. I'm learning this business from Bunny real well, but it's gonna be a while yet. And he was good to take me in, you know? So I say, 'yes, boss,' and 'no, boss,' 'cause he likes that kind of shit. And I get after him about the heart pills, 'cause I don't want him thinking I'm pushing my chances any. But to everybody else, I come across as Bunny's gofer who's got this mind's in the gutter and can't say a sentence without 'fuck' in it somewheres. Nobody's gonna be worried about me competing with them to take over when Bunny goes, and so when it's time I can get them before they even think about getting me."

"I didn't get the impression from Bunny that you guys were in a growth industry. One worth preparing for and protecting against competitors."

"It is if you do it right."

"Meaning kiddie porn, that sort of thing? For the VCR crowd?"

"I don't know nothing about that."

"Then how about an answer to my original question. How the hell did Jane Rust ever get involved with somebody like Coyne?"

Teevens took a minute. "I think maybe for Charlie, this Rust broad was the real thing. But she had another boyfriend, right?"

"Right."

"Guy over to the Redevelopment Authority."

"So I understand."

"Yeah, well, I understand from Charlie that there were some problems there."

"At the Authority?"

"No. Well, maybe. I don't know about that. I'm talking the boyfriend himself."

"What do you mean?"

"The Rust broad told Charlie about it. 'Confidentially,' of course. That fuckin Charlie, he run off at the mouth like a sewer."

"Told him what?"

"About the boyfriend. Seems there was more heat than meat."

"You mean the sex was bad?"

"The worst. The boyfriend just couldn't get it up."

"Impotent."

"That's what they call it."

I left Duckie at the bar and said good night to Bullet-Head at the door. Turning left, I walked to the closest of three liquor stores in sight. I bought a pint of cheap rye whiskey and circled around the block to the mouth of the alley behind the store.

The alley was about fifteen feet wide. I heard some scuffling and laughing down aways. As my eyes adjusted to the moonlight, I could see half a dozen pairs of legs sticking out from behind overflowing dumpsters and overturned trash cans. Then I picked out the source of the sounds.

Three teenagers in matching varsity jackets were playing "keep-away" from a derelict. They tossed a booze bottle one to the other, the victim stumbling from boy to boy, always a toss slow.

I walked down the alley toward them. The kid nearest me, who seemed about my size, stuck his foot out as the bum went blindly by him. Tripping, the derelict sprawled into a pile of loose trash. He slipped a couple of times as he tried to get back up. The laughing got louder.

"What's the joke?" I said.

The nearest kid, the tripper, gave me a quick glance, probably seeing the brown bag in my hand. He said, "Fuck off, hairball. Unless you want to be next."

"Harsh words. But challenging." I came even with Tripper, who squared around to face me. I set my bag on the ground. "There's my bottle, boyo. Who's gonna get the game started?"

Tripper took a step backward, shaking his neck out and using the motion to check the position of his mates. The guy with the original bottle was turning it in his hands, a little shakily I thought. The other kid was looking back up the alley behind him, confirming his line of retreat. I guessed that Tripper was the only initiator in the trio.

"Come on, fellas," I said. "You guys are lettermen, right? I'm just the next level of competition. Who's first?"

Bottle said, "Cliff, maybe we oughta . . ."

Cliff the tripper said, "Shut up."

Edging backward, Retreat looked behind him again.

"Seems to me the team's a little shy, Cliffie. Maybe you've got to lead by example here."

Cliff said, "Why don't you fuck off before we hurt you, man?"

"Hurt me?" I inclined my head toward the derelict in the trash, who was barely moving. "I thought this was just a little game you guys were playing. Just for laughs, you know? I didn't realize you wanted to hurt anybody."

"I'm warning you, man."

"You're gonna have to do better than that, Cliffie."

He tried to. He made like he was turning to review

114

the troops again, but instead brought his right in an uppercut from behind his back. Sucker punch.

I parried it inward with my right palm, shunting my body left and following with a half-force side kick to his stomach. He doubled over and dropped to his knees. I grabbed him by the back of his collar and crab-walked him over to the nearest pile of trash, pitching him forward into it. As he raised back up on all fours, I said, "You get the urge, Cliffie, better to throw up into the garbage."

He obliged me.

I turned to the other two. "Cliffie here got a little too much into the game. Laughed himself sick. You guys feeling queasy, too?"

They shook their heads.

I pointed to Bottle. "Set that down. Gently."

He complied.

"Now, when Cliffie here composes himself, you take him somewhere and clean him up."

Cliff managed to say, "Jesus, guys . . . get me home . . . please."

I moved sideways and gestured toward him. His friends haltingly came forward, each taking an arm and lifting Cliff to his feet. They swung back toward me.

I said, "No. Take him the long way out."

Retreat said, "But our car's—"

"The long way. Or the hard way. Take your pick."

They looked at each other, hefted Cliff a little higher, and took the long way.

I went to the man they'd been razzing. I got him up and over to the comparatively cleaner side of the alley, sitting him against the wall of the adjacent building. "You alright?"

"Why'd she have to go and do that?"

"Who?"

"And with my own son. Hell, I knew she was a slut, they're all sluts. But my own son. Why? Why?"

I retrieved his bottle and mine, resting his lengthways between his knees.

Near the rear door of Bun's, a heap of clothing wearing shoes twitched as I passed. I stopped.

"Hey," I said, shaking the man at the shoulder.

"Go 'way."

I said, quietly, "Hey, pal, I got a pint here for the guy who saw the stabbing the other night."

"Go 'way."

I moved on to the next heap and repeated the offer.

"Seen it. Yeah, yeah. I seen it. Let's have the pint."

I pulled it halfway from the bag, so he could see the label. "Describe the guy with the knife."

"Nigger. Always niggers with the knives. Gimme the pint."

"Describe him."

"Aw, you know the niggers, man. All look alike. Gimme the pint."

"Sorry. No sale."

"Fuck you. Fuck you and the horse you rode in on."

Ten feet farther down, a third body said, "Yeah, I the one seen it."

"Describe the guy."

"Describe him. Charlie be dead."

"I mean the guy with the knife."

"Where's that pint at?"

I showed him.

His face came forward, deep black complexion, lesions on the cheeks, puffy eyes examining the product from a distance of four inches. "Cheap bastard. Couldn't gets no good stuff?"

"I haven't heard much reason to try."

"And you won't, neither. Not for that shit."

"How do I know you're the one I want?"

"Guy you want talked to the cops. You seen anybody else around here makes sense enough, cops talk to him?"

"You still haven't told me anything."

"You wants me to talk, huh? For that cheap shit?"

"Guess we can't do business." I straightened up and turned to move on.

"Wait a minute. Wait!"

I looked down at him.

"Well, come back here. I ain't gone go shouting it all over the alley."

I squatted next to him.

He said, "First thing, what your name be?"

"John Cuddy."

"You ain't no cop."

"No, the cops want information, they just bring you in, dry you out till you feel helpful."

"You gots that right." He put on a cagey grin. "How's about me and you do a little deal here?"

"I told you my name. How about yours?"

"VIP."

"Vip?"

"Vee-Eye-Pee. Very important person. Leastways to you, you showing even that cheap shit there."

"What's the deal?"

"You gives me a little taste, I gives you a little taste."

"I'm guessing your little taste is this pint here."

"Man speaks my language."

"What's my little taste?"

"Something only the man talk to the cops know."

I handed him the pint. He used a corner of his coat to muffle the sound of the top being unscrewed.

"Fuckin bums in this alley, they hears a tax tag

getting tore off, they all over you for some." He glugged half the pint before I stayed his arm.

"You said a little taste for me, too, Vip. Remember?"

"Man done Charlie gots up with Charlie's knife still in his leg. That taste enough for you?"

Bingo. "What's the rest of the deal?"

"This here pint be enough for me tonight. I ain't no fuckin drunk like some peoples I could mention."

"And?"

"And I calls you tomorrow."

"You're gonna call me tomorrow."

"Yeah. You know, like on the telephone?"

"Why can't you just tell me now?"

"'Cause I tells you now, you pays me now. Then I ain't gots nothing by tomorrow 'cause the scum I gots to live with here rip me off."

"What makes you think I'll pay you tomorrow?"

"Watched you with them fuckin white boys up the alley. You the kind comes through. You learns that on the bum, you know?"

I took out the Crestview card I had and wrote my name on it. I put it in Vip's shirt pocket.

"Tomorrow's a long day. When are you going to call me?"

"Don't gots no watch, man. Wanna leave me yours?"

"I don't think so."

"Then be sometime after sun-up. I don't lays around all day like some peoples I could mention."

I rose.

Vip said, "And bring cash money when you comes. You overpaying for this cheap shit I gots to drink."

ELEVEN

Thursday morning broke bright and clear. I opened the window, drawing in deep breaths of ocean air, the seagulls shrieking. I hit the bathroom, then pulled on running shorts, shoes, and a tee shirt Nancy had given me with the legend PUSHING FORTY IS EXERCISE ENOUGH.

Walking by the motel office, I spotted Jones bustling behind the desk. I opened the door and said, "Emil. You're up pretty early."

He looked annoyed. "Goddam receipts."

"What's the matter?"

"I can't find them. I'm the only goddam employee of this chickenshit outfit, and I can't find the goddam receipts book that I musta laid some goddam place." He leaned over the counter. "The hell is that getup?"

"I'm going running. Any jogging trails you can recommend?"

"Jogging trails? You've gotta be shitting me."

"How about just a nice road, reasonably flat, that I can go out about two miles and then come back."

Jones pointed. "You drive west of here yet?"

"No."

"Well, head west along Crestview. The road'll drop toward sea level pretty quick, then she's flat and steady along the water for a while. Take her acrost the river bridge. Other side of the bridge oughta be about two miles."

"Thanks, Emil."

I told him a guy who sounded down and out might telephone for me. Jones groused about it, but finally agreed to take any message.

As I left the office, I heard him mutter, "Jogging trails."

Crestview descended fifty feet, my hamstrings bunching as I thumped downhill. The harbor smell was pungent, probably from the natural human pollution of too many shacks, with too little plumbing, lying in an uneven string along the water to my left. The houses on the other side of the street were bigger though apparently no younger, with the mismatched proportions of the homemade. I counted a trailer about every fourth lot.

There wasn't much vehicular traffic. A cadaverous guy in a baseball cap driving an old yellow pickup waved to me as he headed east. A newsboy with no front teeth on a heavy-frame Schwinn almost collided with me at a hedged driveway. An asthmatic Buick with two primer-painted fenders and a mud-splattered rear end chugged up behind me, passed, and continued around the bend, spewing a noxious combination of oil and smoke out its rope-rigged tail pipe.

You can learn more about an area walking or jogging than driving. I think it's because you have the freedom to appreciate something three or four times from slightly different aspects. A wooden lobster boat, sloughed in a side yard, being cannibalized fore and aft to supply its successor. A dozen lobster pots, the old kind with slat-and-wire construction, rising in alternating tiers on a sagging front porch. Engine parts, heaped in uneven piles outside a double garage with only one door still hinged. A cardboard FOR SALE BY OWNER sign tacked optimistically to a stake in the seared lawn of a plywood cottage with a tin roof.

Halfway through the bend in the road I could see the bridge looming a mile away. A refugee from an erector set, its head and shoulders were covered by a mist the low-angle sun hadn't yet burned off. Picking up the pace a mite, I heard a car with a powerful engine start somewhere behind me. The driver throttled down and seemed to approach, the sound diminishing again. I looked back over my shoulder and saw the front of a Camaro, its amber parking lights watching me from the mouth of the bend. After a minute, I looked again. The car hadn't moved.

I tried to think of what the driver could be doing other than following me. I couldn't come up with anything. On the other hand, he was keeping his distance. Only a quarter mile now from the bridge, I told myself I was imagining things.

I went by a few more houses and a shanty "Open for Breakfast" but hosting only two cars outside it. One was the beat-up Buick that had lapped me earlier. Facing out, its lavish grille gave me a sharklike smile as I went by. The imagination is a bad creature to unleash.

The bridge itself was two lanes, all I-beams and

bolts, rusted here and reinforced there. It looked about a hundred yards long, spanning the shallow river maybe a hundred feet below. There was a steel vertical barrier on the outside walkway of each lane to keep vehicles from sliding off into space. No traffic in sight front or back. I decided to lope along the pedestrian curb anyway.

I was maybe twenty strides onto the bridge when I heard the Buick's engine cough and catch, the driver gunning it to life. I didn't remember hearing the car door open or close, though the morning air was still enough that I should have.

I broke into a sprint for the other side of the river.

The Buick roared up behind me, spitting and choking. I risked a glance. The sun was behind the car, silhouetting the driver as he or she wrenched the wheel to the right, climbing the curb. I was like a bug in a rifle barrel, with the Buick as bullet coming up after me.

Looking forward again, I had at least another fifty yards to the land on the other side of the bridge. Six to seven seconds minimum at the maximum spurt I could manage.

I heard the Buick sand some paint off the side of the bridge. Real close.

Using the barrier part of the bridge as a gymnast's horse, I vaulted up and over. There was six inches of I-beam extruding from the outboard side. My right foot landed and held. The Buick struck the barrier just as my left foot hit, causing me to slide off. The beam barked the skin off my left shin and knee.

Falling, I grabbed for a cross-rung abutment of some kind with my right hand. I couldn't hold on, but it slowed me enough to let me grab and hold the next. Some rarely used muscles popped in my upper arm, but I was able to swing, chimplike, onto another crosspiece with my left hand, getting a purchase with both feet a second later.

The Buick sounded as though it kept going, the wheezing of its engine replaced by the gutty rasp of the other car I'd seen, charging hard, horn blaring. The Camaro came to a screeching halt something short of where I was.

After a car door opened, I heard running steps. Leaning out, I saw a familiar face peering moonlike over the top edge of the barrier.

Duckie Teevens said, "Shit, Cuddy, you look just like Spiderman there."

"You make the driver?"

Duckie shook his head. "I saw the car start up just after you left the motel, but I didn't pay him any attention till I saw him jump the fuckin curb on the bridge." Duckie swiveled toward me and smiled. "I figured he had you sure."

"It was a man, then?"

"Huh?"

"You keep saying 'him' and 'he.' Could you tell it was a man behind the wheel?"

"No way. I think whoever it was had one of those commando hats on, you know?"

"Commando hat. You mean a watch cap?"

"Yeah, those little black things like the kids wear in the snow. Probably was a guy, though."

"Why?"

"Can't see no broad cold-blooded enough to go after you with a car like that."

"Why didn't you chase after him, then?"

Teevens laughed. "I thought you were feeding the minnows. The boss told me, keep an eye on you. Can't keep no eye on you if you're in the water and I'm going after some hit-and-runner, making some kind of citizen's arrest for crissake."

"You peg the Buick as a hit-and-run?"

Duckie slowed for a car turning left, then went around it slowly, using his signal both swerving right and coming back left. He waved to a police car parked in the shadow of a variety store just past the intersection.

"I knew the fucker was there! Thursday morning, he's always there by now. Thinks he was gonna get me, hot car like this. I tell you, I drive them nuts, I do. I got this jet engine under me, I drive like a fuckin grandma. Never got a ticket for nothing, moving violation, equipment, nothing. Fuckers."

"Duckie, you peg the Buick as a hit-and-run?"

He looked over at me. "No. I don't see it that way."

"How do you see it?"

"Seems kinda strange, him lying for you like that, then setting himself up so he could get you on the bridge. Takes a lot of thought, seems to me. Cold mother."

"Also seems kind of strange that Coyne gets himself stabbed, Jane Rust takes an overdose, and the Buick sets up to nail me like that, and they're not connected."

"You're the detective, pal."

"So you still buy your boss's view of somebody acing Coyne as an informant?"

"I can see it."

"If it was your brother Coyne had dropped?"

Teevens got exasperated. "Look, Cuddy, you watch much TV when you were a kid?"

"Some."

"You shoulda paid more attention. That kinda thing happens all the time. Sometimes, a guy turns another guy for money, the first guy don't get to *count* the money, let alone spend any of it."

"And somebody who killed Coyne that way gets Rust to take mashed-up sleeping pills and then tries to spread me over that barrier back there? It doesn't make sense."

"Like I said, you're the detective." He glanced down at my leg. "Looks pretty bad there. You want a doctor?"

"No, thanks. Drugstore'll do it."

Duckie stopped outside a CVS. I went in and bought some antiseptic, bandages, and adhesive tape. Back in the Camaro, there was no talking until we pulled into the motel parking lot.

As I was getting out of the car, he twisted his torso to face me. "Cuddy?"

"Yeah?"

"Something like this happens again, don't bet the mortgage on me being around, okay?"

I looked at him. He said, "I tell the boss about this here, and he's probably gonna tell me to give up tailing you."

I hopped on my right foot and swung the bad leg out of the car. Closing the door, I said, "Thanks for everything so far."

Teevens said, "I mean it," and drove away.

"Christ on a crutch, what happened to you?"

Jones hung back in the doorway to my unit, as I washed away the blood in the tub and swabbed antiseptic on the abraded skin. "Seems jogging's a contact sport down here, Emil."

"Get you anything?"

I motioned toward the items on top of the toilet tank. "I'll be fine with the gauze and all."

"Lemme bring you some breakfast, anyway. Muffins and eggs okay?"

"Great. Thanks."

"Be a few minutes. After all this, gotta check on something first."

"What do you have to check on?"

"Whether you're paid up in advance or not." He turned to go. "Finally found the goddam receipt book."

TWELVE
♦

I finished licking my wounds and ate the breakfast Jones brought me. Getting into a pair of slacks and a sports shirt, I walked stiffly to the car. By setting the seat back farther than usual, I could work the clutch while still being able to control the gas and brake with my right foot.

On the way into town, I stopped and again dialed the office of Richard Dykestra. The receptionist again told me the developer was unavailable. I thanked her and hung up.

Back in the car, I drove until I saw a stationery store on Main Street. I bought a small book mailer and a fancy label. On the label, I wrote Dykestra's name and address. In the upper left corner of the mailer, I printed the name and address of the fictitious Boston law firm of Dewey, Cheatham & Howe.

Then I parked at a meter near the police building. Approaching the front doors, I saw Captain Hogueira in a large, black Oldsmobile, Manos at the wheel. I limped over.

"Mr. Cuddy, you are hurt? We are just returning, but perhaps we could provide you with a ride. This car is one of the few privileges of my rank."

"I'll be alright, thank you. I would like to talk though. Before I see your esteemed colleague Captain Hagan."

In his office, Hogueira said, "How may I be of service?"

"Fair to say the uniformed branch here investigates traffic incidents?"

"With diligence."

"Somebody almost ran me down this morning."

"When?"

"About six-thirty."

"Where?"

"The car followed me from the motel west along Crestview, then tried to resurface the river bridge with me."

"Most unfortunate. Witnesses?"

"One."

Hogueira regarded me for a moment. "Before I inquire of the name of the witness, may I ask why you waited these several hours to report the accident?"

"No accident. The driver was trying to kill me."

"You saw the driver?"

"No. And I didn't get a plate number, either."

Hogueira shrugged. "Of little importance. Almost certainly stolen." His eyes refocused on me. "Again, however, why did you wait so long to contact us?"

"I thought I should bandage myself up first."

"You are injured badly?"

"More in pride than body. I should have seen it coming."

"You should have realized someone would try to kill you with a car?"

"I should have realized that if someone was willing to kill Charlie Coyne and Jane Rust, I probably weighed in as an afterthought."

"Oh, Mr. Cuddy, you should not sell yourself so short. Your presence in our city seems alone to be reordering all kinds of priorities. And speaking of priorities, can you tell me now why you waited so long to report the occurrence of early this morning to the police?"

The Little Prince, who once having asked a question. . . . "I wanted to be sure I'd be reporting it to the right side of the department."

Hogueira breathed laboriously. Not aggravated, just considering things. "Perhaps I should inquire now of the name of your witness?"

"Duckie Teevens. An employee of Bunny Gotbaum."

"Ah, yes. Well, it seems your first impression of the right side of the department is incorrect. This incident certainly seems within Captain Hagan's domain. There is a bench just outside his office where you can await him in relative comfort."

Hagan stumped past me, favoring his right leg. "I can give you five minutes, Cuddy."

I stood awkwardly from the bench, thinking that I hadn't seen him walking the day before. "Old Buick with primered fenders, right?"

He stared at me, his hand on the doorknob to his office. "What are you talking about?"

"Your leg. You got chased by an old Buick this morning, too?"

"Football from high school. Acts up once in a while. You want to see me or not?"

I followed him into the office. We sat down, and I explained what happened to me, including Duckie as witness.

Hagan said, "Sounds to me like your witness is part of your problem."

"More like I'm part of somebody else's problem."

Hagan reclined in the chair, lacing his fingers behind his head. "Guy could have been coming off a bad night. Boss lays him off, he gets soused, maybe mistakes you for the boss."

"Captain, when I was in the MP's, we had a kind of principle we lived by. Know what it was?"

"Can't wait to hear."

"We used to say that nothing happens by coincidence. Everything that seems related is related. Cause and effect, disease and symptom."

"What is this, Philosophy 101?"

"No, it's murder. Two completed, one attempted. No avenging clock-puncher this morning, either. Thoughtful, professional, and damned near successful."

"So you say. And so Duckie boy says. Talk to the sergeant downstairs. He can write up an incident report. That it?"

"Yeah, that's it. Except for one thing."

"Which is?"

"How come you didn't tell me the autopsy report showed Jane Rust was pregnant?"

"I told you that I couldn't see dredging up her problems once she'd decided to end them." Hagan reached for a file on his desk. "Have a nice day, now."

HARBORSIDE CONDOMINIUMS, LTD.
EXPERIENCE A WORLD OF WONDER
LIVING BY THE SEA.
RICHARD DYKESTRA, DEVELOPER

That's what the big sign said. The little sign hanging from the chain link fence was a bit more realistic: THIS IS A HARD-HAT JOB. I pulled the Prelude past the gate and parked behind a Ford Bronco with jumbo tires and a raised suspension. There were plenty of empty spaces around it. I took another look at my book mailer. The hand-printed return address wouldn't fool even a slow secretary, but I figured it could get me onto the job site.

Walking back, I noticed the padlock on the gate was open. I pushed it in.

The site was a countinghouse on an old wharf. The wharf itself, rotting timber pilings and some huge old boulders, didn't seem the most stable foundation for a condo complex. It appeared that Dykestra was going to build his wonderland within the shell of the old countinghouse, since half the exterior filling of the structure had been demolished, leaving only the skeleton of beams and joists that one day would be polished ribs in stylish, fireplaced living rooms. If Harborside were ever finished and successfully sold.

There was very little activity on the site. No crane and wrecking ball to punch out the unwanted parts. I could count only three guys in a far corner, one measuring, two others standing by, leaning on sledgehammers. Day labor is one thing you can't get on credit. Nobody who needs a pay envelope every Thursday's going to stay on the job if wages aren't kept current.

"Hey, you! Can't you read the sign?"

I looked up. A guy wearing construction clothes and a red hard hat stood on a second-floor beam with his fists on his hips like a foreman. He tossed his head toward the gate. "What does that sign say?"

I waved the mailer at him. "I've got something here for Mr. Dykestra."

"Packages go to the office."

"Not this one." I sat down on a fairly flat piece of rubble and crossed my arms.

"I'm coming down." He didn't sound pleased with me.

I lost track of him as he wended his way back into the intact part of the building. He came out a first-floor door along the wharf, with a short, pudgy man in a large-patterned plaid three-piece suit clumping after him. Pudge's vest didn't reach his belt, and his pants didn't reach his shoes.

As they drew even with me, the foreman pushed up his sleeves while Pudge said, "What kind of package you got for Dykestra?"

"Confidential package."

"Give it here."

"You Dykestra?"

The foreman said, "Give the man the package, asshole."

I tried to sound hurt. "I was given explicit instructions to give this only to Mr. Dykestra personally. In hand."

Pudge's jaw set. "In hand, huh? A process server? Al, this guy don't have a hard hat. Throw him off the job before the feds cite me for a safety violation."

"With pleasure."

I figured Al had watched me limp before he yelled at me, and he started for my bad left side. I pivoted on the weak leg, throwing my right hip into his left thigh. Reaching my right arm up and past his left armpit, I threw him over my hip. He landed on his back, the air whoofing from his lungs. My leg hurt as badly as he sounded.

I said, "Mr. Dykestra, someplace we can talk this over?"

Pudge watched me as he said, "Al, you gonna be okay?"

Al, wallowing on the ground, nodded erratically.

Dykestra said, "Let's sit down by the water."

"I gotta say, I figured you'd be around to see me."

"Bruce Fetch give you a call?"

Dykestra laughed. "Bruce is a good guy. He's had more than his share of problems lately, that's all."

"Seems like the kind of town, everybody's got problems."

A man was maneuvering a beamy sea skiff with a small outboard across the choppy bay. He was hunkered down in the stern, spray dousing him every time the prow smacked a wave.

Dykestra said, "You see that boat?"

"Yes."

"What do you see?"

"An old one barely making it."

"That's pretty close to right. The guy in that skiff used to have a big fishing boat. Bank took it from him because the insurance company said the premium's tripled and the bank won't let him go out without insurance to cover their loan. So he loses his boat and now the poor bastard tries to feed his family the only way he knows how, by fishing handlines."

"There a moral to this story?"

"Yeah. Yeah, there's a moral awright. The moral is you gotta change, otherwise you lose what you got and get left with something worse."

"And that's what you're doing here, changing things?"

"Bet your sweet ass. This fuckin town's like a fat broad, you know? Has enough to eat, don't have no reason to look good, it just sits and eats. That's fine, till all of a sudden the food runs out, and nobody thinks the town looks good enough to treat to a dinner."

I looked over my shoulder, partly to view the condo site and partly to watch for Al. "You're a long way from making this look good enough."

"You gotta start somewhere, right? I grew up in Nasharbor. Wrong side of the tracks, wrong side of the sheets. I can't help that. But I got smart the hard way, and I got lucky, too. And now I can do something for the place, give it a hand, help pull itself out of the shit it's in before it gets any deeper."

"And you figure Harborside is just what the doctor ordered?"

"You gotta have some vision. You remember the Faneuil Hall area in the old days?"

"I remember."

"Mud flats, open sewers, wharf buildings so cruddy the rats were looking to move up. Now, what do they get for those waterfront condos? Three, four hundred thousand."

"That's Boston. The city draws young professionals like a magnet. Down here, I don't see people wanting to move into an area that looks like a Soviet missile landed last week. I see them going for single-family homes, bigger, with more property than they could buy in the city."

"Like I said, you gotta have vision. When Harborside hits its stride, other developers'll move on the other parcels around here. Snowball effect, you know?"

"Or Harborside gets built, even though it's a bad tax time and market time for it. Only it's public money fronting the project, so after the construction bookkeeping gets entered, you're made whole. Then if Harborside's a bust, the taxpayers end up paying the tab, as usual."

Dykestra smiled the way a magician does when someone in the audience yells out the secret to a trick he just performed. "I forgot you were listening to that Rust maggot. What other bullshit she throw at you?"

"What difference does it make now?"

"No difference. I just thought I could set you straight on some things is all."

"You ever try to set her straight?"

"Yeah." He got serious. "Yeah, I did try. I tried to show her how what I was doing here was putting people to work, people like that poor bastard in the skiff who won't have to risk drowning himself every day to put food on the table. I tried to show her the plans for this place here, the shot in the arm it'd give the city. Jesus Christ, you'd of thought that she'd get off on that kind of story. But no, man, somebody put a bee up her ass about this and about me. And all my nice talks with her, and even Bruce hosing her, just wasn't making no impression on her. And the shit she was slinging was starting to stick, not because it was true, you understand, but because she just kept slinging it. She was a screwy broad, that one. And I can't say I cried any when I heard she did herself."

"You figure that's what happened?"

"I figure that's what happened."

135

"You know of anything in particular that would set her off?"

Dykestra looked disgusted. "Aw, c'mon, man. Could have been a lot of things. Bruce said he told you about her being pregnant and all. That plus the Coyne guy getting stabbed."

"What do you know about Coyne?"

"Nothing, man. Just from Bruce, that she was real upset about it. Like I said, a screwy broad. I was the editor, I would have fired her."

"You run your own crew here?"

"I run . . . you mean the guys on the job here?"

"Right."

"Yeah. They're my employees. At least, they work for one of my companies. That's public record. Why do you want to know?"

"Any of them drive an old Buick, couple of fenders with just primer on them?"

He didn't look away or stop to think. Maintaining eye contact, he said, "No. Nobody's got that kind of car I ever seen."

I stood up. "Guess that's it for now. Al going to give me any trouble as I leave?"

"Not if I walk you out." Dykestra rose, whisking the dust off the back of his pants with his hands. "'Course, I'm not on the site every day, so I wouldn't stop back here again if I was you."

"Thanks, but I've seen enough."

He shook his head. "You're wrong there, pal. Someday you're gonna think back and say to yourself, 'I saw Nasharbor and Harborside back when.' I'm telling you, this city is perched on the edge of greatness."

I didn't have to ask where I'd heard that before.

THIRTEEN

♦

I left the car in a visitor's spot and walked through the front door of the *Beacon*. The receptionist did not exactly light up.

"I'd like to see Liz Rendall or Malcolm Peete, please."

She told me to have a seat without asking for my name. From the chair, I could see her hissing into her mouthpiece.

It took Arbuckle exactly thirty-four seconds to appear in the archway to the corridor.

"Cuddy, my office."

I followed him back. Glancing around the crowded city room, I couldn't see Peete or Rendall.

Once in his office, Arbuckle motioned toward the chair I'd used the last time. He closed the door behind him hard enough to rattle the glass in the interior window as he marched to his side of the desk.

I said, "Good to show the ranks you're in command."

"What?"

"Slamming the door like that. Good device. Got to be careful not to overuse it, though."

"I thought I told you not to come here after Tuesday."

"You did."

"Then what the hell are you doing here now?"

"You told me to talk with Peete or Rendall. That's who I asked for out front."

"I told you to talk to them on Tuesday. Today's Thursday. Am I going to have to call the cops?"

"I wouldn't. Under the trespass statute, you have to ask me to leave again first. The receptionist heard you tell me to come back with you. Since you're someone in authority on the premises, it seems to me that I'm okay legally."

Arbuckle did a slow burn. He did it well, but I decided not to compliment him.

He said, "Why can't you leave well enough alone?"

"It doesn't look so well to me."

"Can't you see—"

"Aren't you going to ask me about my leg?"

"Your leg?"

"Yeah, I'm limping. Didn't you notice?"

"I don't give a rat's ass about your leg."

"You might be missing a story. Somebody tried to run me down this morning."

"Sounds like a good idea to me."

"It'd be a lot easier if you'd just let me hang around here, ask some questions and look at some files."

"Get out." He banged a button on his phone panel. "Jeannette, if you don't see this guy Cuddy go by you and out within sixty seconds, call the police."

The receptionist's voice came over the speaker box. "And tell them what?"

"Tell them to come get Mr. Cuddy the fuck out of here!"

"Okay, okay."

Arbuckle banged the button again and glared at me. I said, "I hope my knee'll hold up under the strain."

Going through the building's front door, I saw Liz Rendall race up in a little American car with NASHARBOR BEACON on the driver's side door and a CB radio antenna stuck on the roof. She got out and said, "What's wrong with your leg?"

"Hurt it this morning, jogging. Can I speak with you for a minute?"

"Yes, but I'm running late. Wait in your car. I'll be right out."

I went to the Prelude and waited. Two minutes later, she hurried through the door of the *Beacon* and into a different car, an Alfa Romeo convertible. Expensive transportation for a reporter. She started up and drove by, beckoning for me to follow.

Including Rendall, the aerobics class had seven members, all female. The instructor was a muscular woman with short black hair moussed into a spiky brush cut. The tempo was fast, and Liz was the only one in the loft who really could keep up with Spike. The ceiling vibrated with Aerosmith and Whitney Houston while the floor quaked from the cadence of the routines.

Liz wore a yellow leotard outfit with the false socks, in navy blue, that I think are called leg warmers. Slim and sinewy, she moved well, and she knew it. The instructor treated the music as an opponent to conquer. Rendall welcomed the music as a partner to the dance, allowing its excesses to show off her capacity to be both energetic and sensual. I wondered if any of it was for my benefit. I caught myself hoping just a little that it was, which surprised me. Liz looked uncannily like Beth, but she wasn't *like* Beth at all. Liz was more like Nancy, though maybe a little more aggressive.

The tape stopped after forty-five minutes. Rendall grabbed a towel and came over to me. The perspiration scent rolled in front of her, that sweet musk some women exude after hard physical work.

Smiling, she shook her head, the ringlets of hair curling and recurling damply as she rubbed the towel from ear to ear. "You ever try aerobics?"

"No."

"Too sissy for you?"

"Maybe it reminds me too much of another time."

"What other time?"

"When we all wore green and the leader had stripes."

"Then I can't blame you." She passed the towel down her chest, the nipples underneath the stretch material doing their level best to pop out. "What'd you think?"

"I thought you looked great."

Rendall shook her head again, this time negatively. "I don't make myself look good to come here. I make myself come here to look good."

"That's how I meant it."

"Then I'm glad I dragged you along." She grasped my wrist, turning it so she could read my watch. There was a perfectly functioning clock on the wall, but she held tight, as though she were just learning to tell time. "I'm going to have to get out of here. You have a run-in with Arbuckle?"

"Sort of."

"After I came back from lunch with you on Tuesday, he told me he never wanted to see you again. I tried to call you, but all I got was . . ." Liz scrunched her features and dropped her voice two octaves. "'You know, I run a motel here, lady, not some goddam message center.'"

I laughed. "You do a good Emil Jones. How's your Gary Cooper?"

"I'd rather you see my Julia Child. I've got copies of Jane's new articles and my notes on the old ones at home. We can talk over dinner tonight."

"I don't think so."

Her bubbly air subsided. "Look, I don't . . . I have the funeral tomorrow, Jane's, I mean, and I'm kind of down. This," she waved her hand around the loft, "has already started to wear off. I'd really appreciate some company tonight. Even just for dinner. What do you say?"

I thought about how much lousier funerals were when you anticipated them. "Okay."

"Great. Anything you can't eat?"

"Shrimp."

"No problem. You have a good sense of the city yet?"

"Getting there."

"You take Main Street to Armory, then a right onto Armory to The Quay. Follow The Quay all the way to the end. My place is the last one on the right. Seven-thirty, bring white wine." She headed for a makeshift locker room off in a corner.

"Hey, you have a house number?"

"Last place on the right. You can't miss it."

I watched Rendall bounce lightly on the balls of her

141

feet as she moved away. After the folks I planned to see next, a home-cooked meal sounded better and better.

I bought a crabmeat plate and lemonade at a luncheonette, then crisscrossed the east side of town till I found Grantland Avenue. Knocking on doors, I finally got someone to point out Gail Fearey's place. The homes on Grantland made the shacks on Crestview look like the mansions at Newport. What cars there were reminded me of the primered Buick, stilted on cinder blocks or slumped in carports like old dogs.

Fearey's house was a tiny ranch on a narrow lot. The driveway was packed dirt with a few patches of gravel too deeply embedded to erode away. A broken, rusted tricycle was at the edge of the driveway, as though somebody had run over it in the winter and just left it there to degrade over time.

The siding was dull yellow here and flat white there. A picture window had nine frames where there should have been glass. Cardboard, irregularly cut and of different colors, was stapled over four of them. I walked to the front metal door that had neither screen nor storm window. The stock wooden door behind it affected a mail slot. I reached through the metal door and knocked on the wooden one.

On my third try a female voice, husky from too much smoking, spoke from the other side of the door. "Who is it?"

"Gail Fearey?"

"Who is it?"

"Ms. Fearey, my name is John Cuddy. I'm investigating the death of Jane Rust, and I'd like to talk with you."

"I don't wanna talk about her."

"Just a second." I took a twenty from my wallet, tearing it in half. "I'm going to slip half of a twenty dollar bill through the mail slot, Ms. Fearey. You get the other half if you let me come in. You piece the two halves together, the stores will accept it."

No reply.

I flipped the slot and shot the first half in to her.

After a moment, she said, "You got any ID?"

"Yes. Here it comes."

After another moment, the locks clicked and the door itself came open. I pulled the metal door out and stepped inside.

"Here's your ID." She was about five-two and looked anorectic, the big blue eyes popping from a waif's teardrop face like a Margaret Keane painting. Acne scars riddled each cheek, and she used no makeup that I could see. Her lips were bloodless, her clothes a tee shirt that hung off her and jeans that billowed where they should have filled. "Where's my other half?"

"Of the twenty?"

"Right."

"You get that after we talk."

A world-weary expression came over her features. "Sure."

Fearey turned away, walking to a gut-sprung chair. The chair and the daybed sofa across from it had metallic gray electrician's tape in a lot of places. A bulky color TV nearly caved in the milk crates beneath it. The video was on, but no sound came out. A thick elastic band stretched tautly from the ears of the channel changer to a brick on the floor. Sitting, she saw me staring at the set.

"Tuner's gone. Rubber band's the only thing can hold it on a channel."

I chose the daybed sofa. "Is the sound gone, too?"

"No. The brat's asleep in the other room. He's been acting up lately, so keep your voice down, okay?"

"Okay."

"Got a cigarette?"

"Sorry."

"Think I got some somewhere. Just a second."

Fearey shuffled to the kitchen counter, pushing a Burger King bag onto the floor before finding a crushed pack of something. She pawed through three drawers for matches.

Coming back and lighting up, she said, "I'm trying to quit. For the kid. Bad for his lungs too, they say now."

I nodded. "I understand you lived here with Charlie Coyne."

"No."

"No?"

"No. He lived here with me."

"The difference being?"

"This house was my parents'. They died, and I got it. Charlie, he never owned anything in his life."

"How'd you meet him?"

"Charlie?"

"Yes."

"I thought you wanted to know about Rust, the reporter."

"I do. I think her death and Charlie's are connected."

Fearey almost laughed. "They were connected alright."

"I heard that too, but I don't understand it."

She looked around. "You mean you don't under-

144

stand how he could leave me and all this every coupla nights to hump Miss College Tight-Ass?"

After thinking about my phrasing, I said, "I guess I mean I don't see how they would have become interested in each other."

"Thanks for sparing my feelings like that."

I didn't say anything.

"Look, Charlie, he wasn't much, you know? But there was something about him. He just had a look in his eyes, like to say, 'I really know how to make a woman happy.' I don't know how else to describe it, because it never made sense to me, either, and I was nuts about the guy."

"Jane Rust told me that Charlie was her confidential source for a story on pornography. Kiddie porn."

"Charlie did all kinds of things. I never got involved."

"I'm not saying you did. I just need to know what was going on."

"Can't help you."

"Charlie a delivery boy for the stuff?"

The lips dissolved into two traced lines. "Like I said, I can't help you."

"Know anybody who can?"

"No."

"The night Charlie was killed. Tell me about it."

The lips relaxed, and she looked past me, out the window. "We had dinner here, some Kentucky Fried he bought on the way home. Tiger's favorite."

"Tiger?"

"The kid. Charlie's and mine. He's two. Charlie called him Tiger, help make him tough, you know?"

I was thinking that half the people in the city were named after animals, but I said, "Go on."

"Well, we had the chicken, and Tiger got the runs,

he gets them sometimes from the fast-food stuff, don't know why, and Charlie, he'd had a few beers and wasn't about to sit around all night, smell the brat's shit every ten minutes."

"When did he leave here?"

"I don't know. Around 'Wheel of Fortune.'"

"The game show?"

"Yeah."

"So maybe seven, seven-thirty?"

"Around there."

"Do you know where he was going?"

"The Strip."

"He said that?"

"No, but that's where he always went."

"Any particular place?"

"Yeah. Anywhere they shook tits and ass. Charlie was a consistent son of a bitch."

"Bun's?"

"One of his favorites."

"Because he got comped to drinks?"

"If that means free ones, that's Charlie, alright."

"Charlie drink heavily?"

"Charlie did everything 'heavily.' He found out early in life that if you can get enough booze, drugs, and sex, the rest don't bother you so much."

"How did you find out he was dead?"

Fearey looked past me again. "The cops. The fuckin cops. They roar up to the house, sirens and lights. I don't have a phone, but Christ, they'd coulda called a neighbor first, couldn't they? They didn't have to come tear-assing up here like it was a bust or something."

"You go with them?"

"Yeah. This fat sergeant, he said they needed me to identify the body. Bastards!" Her voice rose. "Tiger's screaming his lungs out from the noise and all the strange people. Half the street's out on their lawns, shaking their heads at the fuckin lowlifes brought the cops down. Like they never had a cruiser come to their house, right?"

I heard a cry from the next room. Fearey said, "Shit. Just a minute."

She stubbed out her cigarette and went down the hall. Left alone, I noticed something odd about the tape on the furniture.

Fearey returned shortly, hefting a little kid with just a diaper pinned on him. A smear on his cheek looked like jelly, but then anything on a kid's face looks like jelly. Tiger took one look at me and whipped his head back into his mother's breast.

"He'll be okay. Just don't raise your voice or you'll get him crying."

"I'll do my best. You hear from anybody after Charlie's death?"

Fearey tightened. "Hear from anybody?"

"Yes. Charlie worked for Bunny Gotbaum, right? Anybody come by?"

She shook her head. "Bunny Gotbaum ain't exactly General Motors, you know? They don't have no benefit plans or anything like that down on The Strip."

I fingered the taping on the sofa.

Fearey said, "What are you doing? Leave that alone there."

"Tape looks pretty new."

"Yeah, we change it every coupla weeks for guests."

"What I mean is, the tape all looks new. On all the furniture. Even with a two-year-old running around the house."

No response.

"Like it was all taped at the same time. Like because it all got ripped up at the same time."

"That's none of your business."

"When you got back that night, after the police and Charlie, I mean. This place was wrecked, wasn't it?"

"This place is always wrecked. I'm not much into housework."

"I mean it was torn apart by somebody, like by somebody looking for something."

She nuzzled the child, speaking more softly. "I left Tiger with a neighbor down the street. Old woman, nice enough to come up, see if I needed help with the cops and all. So there wasn't anybody here when I went off with them. Musta been two, three hours later when I got back. The cops dropped me at her house, I picked up Tiger, then walked over here. I opened the door and . . . I didn't know what to do. The place was destroyed, the furniture, the closets, even the stuff from the refrigerator was all over the floor in there. Why'd they have to do that?" She started to cry softly. "We didn't have shit. Why'd they have to do that?"

I waited a minute, then said, "Can I ask you a couple more questions?"

Fearey wiped her nose on the child's shoulder. "Ask."

"Was there anything that they could have been looking for?"

"Like what?"

"Anything Charlie might have been holding for Jane Rust?"

"I don't know what you're talking about."

"Documents, photos, videotapes. Anything."

"You mean the porn stuff again."

"Right."

"Look, I already told you. I don't know nothing about any of that, alright?"

"Alright. Do you know a man named Bruce Fetch?"

"No."

"He was Jane Rust's boyfriend before she became involved with Charlie."

"Oh, him. Yeah. She talked to Charlie about him, and Charlie'd say things to me. I never met the guy, though."

"Charlie told you about Fetch?"

"Mister, Charlie told everybody about everything. That's why this confidential source shit is so stupid. Charlie was about as confidential as a loudspeaker."

"Did Bruce Fetch know about Charlie being Jane Rust's lover?"

"I don't know, but like I said, Charlie shot off his mouth about everything, it wouldn't surprise me if Charlie told him himself."

I said, "Ms. Fearey, on the level, what do you think happened?"

She raised her voice angrily. "What do I think happened?"

The child began to cry. I said, "Yes."

"What I think happened is that bitch reporter got Charlie killed somehow." The child began to wail. "Shut up, Tiger! I think that bitch got him to fall in love with her, really in love. She screwed him up so much he did something so stupid he couldn't get out of it." The child was screaming now. "I said to shut up! God, none of this would've happened if I'd stayed with the Duck."

"What?"

"Never mind."

"Who did—"

149

"Get fucked." The child was shrieking hoarsely now, and Fearey struggled to her feet. "Get out! Get out of here!"

I left the other half of the twenty on the sofa. "We're square. I'm sorry about Charlie."

She followed me to the door, the child nearly drowning her out. "Yeah, yeah, you're so sorry, do me a favor, okay?"

"If I can," I said, going through the door.

"That Rust bitch. She in the ground yet?"

"Tomorrow. The funeral's tomorrow."

"Yeah, well here's what you can do. You can hawk up a good one and spit on her fuckin grave for me."

Fearey kicked the door shut behind me.

FOURTEEN

$\diamondsuit$

"If you so much as touch Bruce, I'm calling the police."

I smiled politely at Grace and said, "He swung on me last time. Can you let him know I'm back?"

She didn't return the smile. "Wait right here."

Entering Fetch's office, she closed his door behind her, then reappeared, looking even less happy. "He'll see you, but remember what I said about the police."

"I will."

Fetch was seated at the computer terminal, an architectural drawing turned sideways on the monitor's screen. There was a splint on his right ring finger.

He said, "What do you want now?"

I took a seat in front of the desk, causing him to swivel around to face me. "Same questions as last time, but this time I'd like some better answers."

"I already told you everything I know."

"Not quite. Let's start with Charlie Coyne. You knew he was Jane's substitute lover, didn't you?"

"No."

"Doesn't wash, Bruce. Jane told you about Coyne being her confidential source."

"You don't know what you're talking about."

"I think I do. She didn't share things with her editor, that's for sure. Jane was pretty distraught by Monday afternoon, and after I pushed her some, she admitted talking it over with a couple of people, people she trusted. That would have to include you."

Fetch sneered, but not very convincingly. "Sure, Jane's gonna tell me the name of the guy who's replacing me?"

"No. No, I don't see it that way. I see it more like Jane needing to talk with someone about her professional problems, and my guess is she just told you about Coyne as her source. You're the one who put two and two together."

"You're crazy."

"My guess is it made you crazy, thinking about them together, especially given the kind of guy he was."

"Bullshit."

"Or maybe Coyne himself told you about them. Bragged to you about how much he satisfied her by comparison."

"Goddammit! I told you, I had the mumps so I'm—"

"Sterile not impotent. I know. It's just that Coyne was spreading a different story."

"You fucking bastard."

"And speaking of which, then to realize he was the father of her baby—"

"Look!" Fetch leaped up. "When Coyne got killed,

I didn't even know Jane was pregnant! Hell, she didn't know, just thought the stress and all had fouled up her cycle somehow."

"Which still leaves you with a pretty strong motive for killing Coyne when he got stabbed, because he was cutting in, humiliating you. Then a stronger motive to kill Jane, when you realized she was carrying his child."

He brought the injured hand to his face, but winced from a pain that went beyond the finger. "I loved her, for God's sake. Why can't you see that? I loved her."

"What kind of car do you drive, Bruce?"

"What?"

"Your car. What make and model?"

"The hell difference does that make?"

"I'm just curious. Save me a trip to the Registry."

Fetch seemed to give in, sinking back into his chair. "Ford. Station wagon. Satisfied?"

"Big one?"

"The car?"

"Yes."

"I guess so. Country Squire. I bought it used off my brother when he was getting a new one. Why do you care about all this?"

"Monday night, the night Jane died, you went to her house, didn't you?"

"No!"

"Bruce, I know your car was there."

"I wasn't there, and it wasn't there."

"It was late. You have a date planned with her?"

"No."

"Reconciliation, maybe?"

"No. Look, why don't you get out of here?"

"Not until I get the truth. You loved her? Seems to me you'd be interested in finding out who killed her."

"She killed herself, remember? Suicide, you know?"

"I don't think so. I think somebody mashed up some pills, a lot of pills, and put them in her cocoa. She didn't take pills generally, so she'd have no way to judge the potency of the dose from the taste. I think somebody stayed there for a couple of hours, searching the place very carefully and systematically for something, something that wasn't found at Coyne's house the night he died and it was ransacked. I think that person sat with Jane, sat and watched her die very slowly from the pills, just slip further and further—"

"Stop it! Stop it now!"

Without knocking, Grace opened the door. "Are you alright, Bruce?"

"Yes."

She treated me to a murderous glare. "Are you sure?"

Fetch said, "Yes, yes. Leave us alone, okay?"

Reluctantly, she drew back and closed the door.

I said, "You drove there Monday night, didn't you?"

"Uh-huh."

"Why?"

"I knew—I knew she'd been under a lot of pressure, that things weren't going any better at the paper, especially since Coyne died. She blamed me . . . no, that's not fair. She didn't want to blame me for him being killed. She didn't want to believe I told anybody about Coyne being her source."

"Did you?"

"Tell anybody, you mean?"

"Yes."

154

"No, I didn't."

"You're sure."

"I'm sure."

"Did Jane tell you who else she discussed Coyne with?"

"No. She said it was better I didn't know, like she was some kind of spy or something. I couldn't believe that she thought the guy was going to help her or anybody else. I kind of knew who he was . . . that is, I'd seen him down at . . . down on The Strip once in a while. I went down there . . . to get stimulated, you know? To see if the . . . shows and all could help me that way."

"Go on."

"Well, one night at this place, a bar called Bun's, he comes up to me between . . . between shows and sits down and starts telling me, telling me to my face about how him and Jane . . . made love. About what she said while he was . . ."

I gave him a moment. "How did Coyne know who you were?"

"He said from the picture."

"Picture?"

"Yeah. At Jane's house. She had a photo of her and me together. On her dresser."

"That night at Bun's, you guys fight it out?"

"No. No, I was . . . too ashamed, I guess. I just ran out of there, never went back. Then Coyne gets killed maybe a week later, and Jane suspects, well, like I said."

"So why did you go to Jane's on Monday night?"

"I was home, drinking. I don't . . . don't drink well. I got a little high, and I started calling her. I'm not sure what I was thinking, I guess that I could convince her to take me . . . to give us another try as a couple. Well, I called her, I don't know, four or five times, and let it ring out, no answer. So finally I pulled on some sneakers and sweat clothes, and went out to my car, figure to see her face to face but be dressed casually, you know? Like it was a spur-of-the-moment kind of idea."

"When she wasn't home?"

"Huh?"

"You expected to see her at her house when she hadn't been answering her phone?"

"Oh, no. I . . . I thought maybe she had somebody else now. Somebody else like Coyne. Every time the phone rang and she didn't answer that's what I . . . pictured in my head. Anyway, I finally got mad enough to drive there. I still . . . I still had a key to her front door. She gave it to me because the buzzer bothered her landlady."

"What time was this?"

"I don't know. Late, maybe eleven-thirty, midnight. I shouldn't even have been driving, what I'd had to drink. Anyway, I open the door to her place, and the stereo is going, and so I sneak around to the bedroom, to sort of peek in I guess, I didn't really know what I was doing, and then I see her. . . ." Fetch put his good hand up to his eyes. "She was just lying on the couch, like she'd fallen asleep. I touched . . . I touched her, and she was cold, and there was this smell, like a clogged toilet, and I realized she . . . she was dead. I . . . I'd never seen anybody dead like that. I panicked, I suppose. I remember running toward the front door. And I remember jumping in the car. And that's all. Except for being scared, every day after that."

"Scared about what?"

"About what? About finding Jane's body and not reporting it or anything."

"But you figured she'd committed suicide, right?"

"I didn't know what to think, understand? I mean, all I knew was she was dead. I didn't look around for anything or anybody. I just knew she was dead. It was only when I got back home and stopped shaking that I realized she probably died of something like that. Suicide, I mean. The way she looked, no blood or anything, I never even thought about murder."

"Tell you what."

"Huh?"

"Think about it now."

Connie eyed me suspiciously as I approached her window.

I said, "Can you get Duckie for me?"

She put her *People* magazine down carefully, saving her place. "You're getting to be a real pain in the ass."

"Pretty please with sugar on it?"

Connie reached under her counter, then made a ceremony of bringing the magazine back up so I couldn't see her face anymore. My loss.

Aside from four insurance salesmen whooping it up at the bar, Duckie Teevens and I were alone in Bun's. He'd suggested we take a table off in a corner. Sherry, who seemed to double as daytime waitress, at least for Duckie, took our order. Neither of us said anything until she'd delivered the drinks, whiskey for Duckie and a Michelob for me.

Teevens clinked his glass against the neck of my bottle and said, "So you wanted to talk with me, talk."

"I haven't noticed you over my shoulder for a while."

"Like I told you, Bunny decided he didn't want me trailing you no more."

"Can you tell me why?"

"I figure that's his business."

"No question you knew Coyne was seeing Jane Rust before he died, right?"

"We told you that, Bunny and me."

"So you did. About the same time you couldn't quite remember Gail Fearey's name. And address."

Duckie darkened. "That's right."

"Funny thing about that. She remembers you pretty clearly."

"Yeah?"

"Yeah. She said she used to go with you, and she's lived in the house there for a long time, used to belong to her parents."

"So?"

"So I'm wondering why the failure of memory from a guy who seems to have everything else pretty straight."

Teevens played with his glass, making the little circles again. "Supposing I don't feel like talking about that?"

"Feel like listening?"

He shrugged.

I said, "You remember pretty well what Gail Fearey looked like some time ago, before she got hooked up with Coyne. I'm thinking that her going for him bothered the hell out of you. Duckie Teevens was trying to make something of himself. The wrong way, maybe, but at least you were going forward. Charlie Coyne was a bum, and you knew it, and it burned you that she couldn't see it."

Duckie spoke to his whiskey. "She could see it."

"She just couldn't do anything about it."

"That's right. Charlie had that, I gotta admit. He had the magic somehow. I never could see it, but the broads sure did."

"I'm wondering why your boss would have hired old Charlie."

"What do you mean?"

"Well, it's pretty clear Gotbaum looks on you like a son."

"Yeah?"

"Yeah, which makes it odd to me that he'd hire Charlie who cut you out from a girl you liked."

Teevens emptied his glass and tapped it on the table top. Sherry came over immediately.

She said, "You want another, Duckie?"

"That's what I want."

"Kinda early, ain't it?"

"Another."

"You got it."

Teevens waited till the second drink arrived, though he didn't take any of it. After Sherry went back to the insurance crowd, he said to me, "I asked the boss to put Charlie on."

"Why?"

"Because Charlie was living with Gail, and she was raising his kid, and they needed the money. And sure as shit nobody else was gonna go out of their way to recruit the guy."

"Charlie was delivering the porn tapes, right?"

"I told you, I don't know nothing about that."

"You're in the business of showing films, Duckie. Dirty pictures. Only it's a dying trade, like Bunny told me. 'The VCR's, they're wiping me out,' he said. But you still want to move into the business. Only one way that works. You don't have the resources to open a legitimate chain of video stores, and the ones already

159

out there offer most of the kinds of movies you'd have anyway. Except the forbidden fruit, right?"

"You're fulla shit."

"The kiddie stuff, Duckie. Maybe snuff or fake snuff films, too. The kinds of things the suburban fathers can't quite ask the wife to pick up on the way home from school with the kids."

He downed half the second drink.

"Only to move that kind of stuff, you have to be careful, selective, even secretive. So Charlie Coyne is the mule, carrying the stuff around, customer to customer or maybe club to club. Is that how it works, Duckie? The guys get together in a club to sort of pool their capital and swap their favorites?"

Teevens took a deep breath, then let it out and spoke low and quietly. "The fuck do you know about it?"

"Only that I see you with a pretty strong motive for killing Charlie. He gets caught in the net with the wrong kind of movies, and he gets intimate with the wrong kind of reporter, a crusader who thinks she can use him to bring down businesses like yours through her newspaper, bring down the future you've put in ten years to inherit."

"Twelve years. I been with the boss twelve years."

I didn't say anything.

He said, "The way you figure it, the same guy who killed Charlie killed the reporter girl, right?"

"Right. And then ripped the hell out of Gail Fearey's place looking for something."

"What?"

"The night Charlie was stabbed, somebody ransacked Gail's house, took a knife to most of the furniture. Looking for something."

"I didn't know about that."

"You didn't."

"Not about the searching there, no."

"But you were here the night Charlie was killed in the alley."

"I was here. I told you that."

"Where were you Monday night?"

"Monday night. That's when the reporter OD'd, right?"

"Maybe with some help."

Duckie said, "Then you got problems."

"I've got problems?"

"Yeah. If the same guy did Charlie and the girl, the guy can't be me."

"Why not?"

"Monday, Bunny had a bad spell. The heart shit, you know?"

"Go ahead."

"Well, on Monday night, Sherry and me was sitting with him for maybe four or five hours in the hospital over to Fall River there."

"You were."

"That's right. With maybe a dozen docs and nurses and gofers mobbing the boss and us."

"What time was this?"

"Time? I dunno. No, wait. The spell come over him during the second feature, so maybe seven-thirty, eight o'clock. The hospital there, it'd have when we rolled in. We was there till after midnight, Sher and me. And even after the boss was okay, they said he'd still have to stay the night. Sher was feeling sad and all, so I took her back to my place and consoled the fuckin shit out of her."

I watched him. Sherry wasn't exactly a solid alibi,

but the rest was a stupid story to trot out if it wasn't true. He finished the whiskey and rose, not bothering to leave any money on the table.

"Ask Sher, you want to. She'll remember. They always remember how the Duck makes them happy."

FIFTEEN

◆

The elder Schonstein violated the first rule of being a cop. He listed himself in the telephone directory.

I arrived at the address just after five. It was a modest Cape, two dormers on the second floor and a breezeway connecting a one-car garage. The breezeway had a concrete ramp sloping gently up to the side door of the house itself. In the driveway was a five-year-old predecessor of Hogueira's Olds staff car, highly polished. The stoop to the front door looked newly poured or little used. I rang the bell.

When the door opened, I had to look down for the voice that said, "Who are you?"

The man was in a wheelchair, a stadium blanket across his lap, legs, and right hand. His left index finger hovered over buttons on the arm of the chair. Bald, his eyes hid under a craggy brow and above a still-jutting jaw.

"Mr. Schonstein?"

He said, "Yeah, but Schonsy suits me better. You gonna answer my question?"

"My name's Cuddy, John Cuddy. I'm—"

"I know who you are. With everybody talking about you, I wondered how long it'd be before you got around to me."

"I was surprised to find you in the phone book."

"Wouldn't do much good not to be. Everybody knows where I live."

"I'd like to ask you some things."

"I expect you do. Well, come on in before I get a crick in my neck looking up at you."

Schonstein pressed a button on the armrest, the chair emitting a low whine and turning him into the house. I entered and closed the door behind me. Following him into the living room, I saw an old-fashioned plush sofa with pine coffee and end tables. A big oxblood Barcalounger was centered six feet from a large-screen television. Next to the lounger, newspapers were heaped, with the folds zigzagged, like bricks in a tower built to go as high as possible without tumbling over.

"'Scuse the mess, but being in the chair and all, it's just easier to leave the damn papers like that. My son comes by once a week or so and cleans 'em out for the scouts."

"The scouts?"

"Boy scouts. Used to be a troop leader myself. The scouts collect the papers, and somebody helps out with hauling them to a recycling plant somewhere." He tipped his head toward the couch. "Sofa's probably the best seat in the house for you. Don't use it much myself, so watch you don't choke on the dust."

I sat down, the cushions enveloping me. I could

imagine why he didn't use it. Once in, he'd have a hell of a time levering himself up and out again.

"Comfy?"

"I would be if you let go of what you've got under the blanket."

Schonstein grinned, teeth a mile too perfect for the rest of the face. Bringing his hand into view, he looked down, rolling the Browning automatic first left, then right, as though it were being featured in an advertising video. With thirteen in the magazine and one in the chamber, it would be a while before he'd have to reload.

"Mark said you were a pretty sharp fella."

"Doesn't take a genius to figure an ex-cop's gonna answer the door with some backup."

"'Specially some old fuck in a wheelchair, huh?"

"Especially."

"You might just be alright, boy. I can see how you could of knocked Mark off his stride a bit."

"The chair. From the disability?"

"Uh-huh. Damnedest thing. Come through Korea without a scratch, not even frostbite. Re-upped once, then twenty-eight years on the force here, not much more bumps and bruises than a bad sleigh ride. Until four years ago. I'm heading home after a midnight tour when I see smoke pouring out of this four-family, edge of a Porto neighborhood. They're good people, mostly, but they get stiff as fish from that red piss they drink. I figure I better see what's going down.

"Then I see this kid at the third-floor window. He's big enough to know he's in the shit, but small enough, he doesn't know what to do about it 'cept scream his lungs out. So I kick in the front door, taking the steps two at a time and banging every door I pass. People run outta there like ants from a hill. You couldn't count 'em all. One of the women, girl actually but they start young, you know what I mean, one of them had the balls to follow me up the steps, yelling something I couldn't catch. Funny how you can live among 'em for so long, never get the hang of their talking.

"So her and me hit the top floor, there's serious fire 'round us now, can't barely breathe much less see for shit, and I had to damn near knock the door off the hinges anyway to get us in. Smoke's worse somehow, but she gets hold of a little baby, and I grab the kid at the window, and we start down. She was hell-bent scared, but she knew the stairs and I didn't. Damned landing, they never nail the runners down right, suppose I shoulda been surprised there was any there at all. I catch my heel in it, going full tilt down, and tear the shit out of one knee while I'm breaking my fall with the other leg, all the time trying to keep the kid's head from cracking open on the steps. I got all the way down, but it felt like somebody'd taken a bat to my legs, and the boys in one of our units had to carry me out like a dime-a-dozen halfback."

"Hell of a story."

"Damned right."

"You have surgery on the knee?"

"Knees. Both of them. Wanna see?"

You can retire them, but you can't keep the good ones from sensing where you're going. "So I can check for recent knife wounds?"

Schonstein grinned again, but reached down to his cuffs, inching up the pants legs like a demented stripper until I could see the old stitch tracks. The calves looked toned instead of withered, but there were no new marks or scars.

He said, "Satisfied?"

"Some."

Schonstein dropped his trousers back to normal. "Good. Good to be a bit skeptical, I mean. Lotsa cops forget that these days."

"The motorized chair help?"

"Godsend. I figured I'd only be in this thing for two, three weeks, then braces, cane, and back to normal. But it didn't work out that way. Barely ever got to use the braces. Docs said it was the arthritis. Always had some twinges going back to my thirties, never paid it much mind till the surgery and all sort of speeded things up. But I get by, I get by."

"You're still able to drive?"

"The car you mean? Hell, yes. The department— actually the city council technically, I guess. The boys let me bid on it when they were selling the fleet to buy new ones. Damned fine car, big engine, best suspension, which makes a difference when you feel the potholes a little more now. Had a guy alter it for me, makes it easier to drive with just the hands. Probably be my last car, too, but that's alright. Saved the best for last."

"Mind me asking about an earlier car?"

"Figured that's why you're here. Gotta give you credit for patience, though. Patience, that's the most important thing for an interrogation, you know. Skepticism and patience, they're in short supply on the force now."

"That night with Hagan and the boy who was killed. Can you tell me your version?"

"No, but I'll tell you what happened, you don't get too puffed up with all my compliments there."

"I'll try not to."

Schonstein slid the Browning under the blanket, rotating his shoulders on the back of the chair. "Neil and me were in the cruiser, regular patrol. He was on the job maybe eight, ten months. No, eight, eight sticks in my mind. It was summertime, we were doing the four to twelve, nice and easy. Not too hot, not too much humidity, no real reason for anything to happen. We turn a corner two blocks off The Strip, Neil's at the wheel, and we go by an alley. I see this skinny kid in blue jeans and a tee shirt playing with the back door of a store. Well, you don't have to be no fortune-teller to know what he's getting ready to do, so I tell Neil to turn right, and I reach for the passenger side spot. I flip it on, the kid's off and running like a deer. Neil had this bad knee from football, lucky he passed the physical with it, so after he takes the cruiser as far as it can go, I get out and sprint after the little fuck. He's maybe five-ten, one-forty dripping wet if he ever took a bath, which I doubt. But he ain't no Olympic threat, and I catch up to him just as he stumbles and goes down near this abandoned building. I didn't see any weapon, so I don't pull mine. I just reach down for him, but when I lift him up by the left arm, he's got this brick in his right, and he bashes in my nose. How many times your nose been broke?"

"Twice."

"Yeah, it looks it. Well, I had mine busted maybe three times before this, but they didn't hurt like this one. I just plain wasn't ready for the pain. It was like a killer wave crashing onto a beach in a storm. It put me down and near out. Then the kid comes down with it again, and almost tears my cheek off, over here." Schonsy tapped under his right eye. "I was about out of it when Neil tackled him. I mean, those days, no question he coulda just shot the kid. But no, he tries to be the good cop, take the kid without deadly force, and the kid falls funny and breaks his fuckin neck.

Neil realizes the kid's dead and breaks down. He was like that, too sensitive for the damned job, I thought then. But he don't know what all to do, so I tell him, pick up the kid and bring him to the cruiser, we gotta radio, alert the hospital. So Neil picks the kid up like he was somebody's new baby, me shagging my ass out of the alley. Lucky I had the sense to bring the brick he used. We called it in, then headed to the emergency room."

"Justifiable."

"No question. For God's sake, the kid was braining me with a brick. Neil could've put six into him, and even today, with the damned shooting teams and paperwork and plaintiffs' lawyers like bucks around a bitch, it woulda been a good shot. What got the guy in trouble was he tried to take the kid without a gun, like I said."

"What kind of trouble?"

"Oh, just the usual newspaper shit. The department, the city, everybody backed him on it. Lucky we had a camera of ours at the hospital, they got some shots of me with more blood coming out than a butchered cow. But the papers still played it up, and the kid's mother tried to start some shit, but nobody paid her much mind, and that was that."

"The mother still around?"

Schonstein flapped his lips. "Wouldn't know."

"Would you remember her name?"

"Probably not."

I said, "The mess doesn't seem to have held Hagan back much."

"Why the hell should it? That's what really burns me, you know? That's what woulda driven me off the force, the knees hadn't done it first. You're a cop, you spend half your time locking up guys you know are gonna be on the street before the end of the shift, you gotta be so careful to say 'alleged' and 'supposed' so you don't violate their rights to a fair trial, and then when they get a trial it's about as fair as the Celtics playing a school-ground team, the way the system's rigged for the guilty. So they get off entirely. Or, if they do get convicted, the judge hands them three to five, which means maybe eighteen months if they don't try to fuck the chaplain, and then we're not supposed to single them out once they're released. We're supposed to treat them like they paid their debt and all. Well, how about us, huh? When a cop like Neil saves his partner's life, and I'm telling you that's what happened here, he saved my fuckin life for me. When a cop does that, and he hurts the perp by accident, by accident now, and it comes down as justifiable, how come that has to drag him down for the rest of his life, huh? Why the fuck is there one standard for them and a different one for us? Tell me that."

"How about you tell me about your son, instead."

"He's a good cop."

"I've seen how he is as a cop."

Schonstein pretended I meant what he meant. "Then what else you want to know?"

"Strike you as just a little odd that your son and his partner Cronan both have corroborated alibis for the night Charlie Coyne was killed?"

"No, it don't. I spent twenty-eight years scraping the Charlie Coynes of this city outta car wrecks and gutters. Pieces of shit like Coyne die as regular as old folks in a nursing home. You know you're gonna lose a couple this week, you just don't know which one's gonna go any particular night, that's all."

"Without Coyne, your son couldn't be indicted."

"With Coyne, I don't see how they're gonna prose-

170

cute him, either. Look, I understand you talked with the Rust girl about this before she took the pills, right?"

"Right."

"Well, I didn't know the woman myself, except to see her across the room once in a while, but I hear she wasn't too tightly wrapped, you know?"

"I know what you mean."

"Sure you do. Well, what she believed, what Coyne maybe told her she oughta believe so he could get his dick wet, that don't necessarily add up to what happened, get me?"

"You mean your son didn't have his hand out."

Schonstein's face clouded, and I got a sense of what a terror he must have been on the street. "That's what I mean, boy. When I come on the force here, how many Jews you figure they have in uniform?"

"No idea."

"None. I got back from the service, I was a veteran, they didn't like it but they didn't have a choice. The law was clear as a bell on that one. If it's alright with you, we can skip over the things they wrote on my locker and car in those days, and the jack-offs they partnered me with. Took maybe five years for me to whale the shit out of every guy wanted to know how tough I was. I got through that, things were okay. Better than okay. There was a time when the cops ruled this city, boy, the way it's supposed to be done. And I was part of it. But then with the Supreme Court and the lawyers and all, somehow it all just slid into the shit. The laws never did protect the citizens, but now not even the cops can."

"You got a point in here somewhere?"

The face got darker, then he burst out laughing. "You don't swallow the bull too quick, do you."

"Not if I can help it."

"Well, see if this goes down a little easier. Coyne said Mark was on the pad from Bunny Gotbaum, right?"

"That's how I heard it."

"Alright, you're Schonsy's son on the force here, you figure Mark's gonna take money from another Jew? When his father had to whip half the force to get any respect as one himself?"

I said, "You know Gotbaum?"

"I know him. Uniforms don't cover vice here, but I know him."

"I mean from growing up around here."

"Why?"

"Seems to me you're about the same age, same religion, reasonable you knew each other as kids."

"Yeah, we knew each other. No temple or nothing for either of us, but we were only a grade apart in school."

"You ever introduce Mark to Gotbaum, maybe?"

"Working vice, Mark would have met him on his own. Believe me."

"Most of the time."

Schonstein seemed tired. "You got any more questions?"

"They ever figure out what started it?"

Just a glimmer of understanding before he set his face for confusion. "How's that?"

"The fire?"

"My . . . the one where I got hurt, you mean?"

"Uh-huh."

"Naw. Nobody died, and nobody fessed up. Why?"

"You ever think about suing?"

"For getting hurt helping a kid? You kidding?"

"You must have thought about it."

"No."

"Who owned the building?"

"You're better than I thought, boy."

"You going to save me a trip to the paper and the tax assessors?"

"Take you a few more steps than that, the way I hear he's got his corporations and trusts stacked one on top of the other."

"And if I sort of kept unstacking them till I got to the bottom?"

"You'd find another local who made good."

"Named?"

"Richie Dykestra."

"And you didn't think about suing him?"

"Didn't have to. He settled with me. Fair and square. No damned lawyers involved."

I stood up. "I can see myself out. Thanks for your time."

As I reached the door, Schonstein said behind me, "Gonna have to watch out for you, son. Yes, I will."

SIXTEEN

◆

It was muggy when I left Schonstein's. Not being due at Liz Rendall's until seven-thirty, I drove back to the motel, showered, and changed. I reminded Emil as obliquely as possible that I might be getting a telephone call from Vip. Emil reminded me that he wasn't no goddam message center and that he hadn't gone goddam senile since the first time I'd mentioned it.

I found a decent bottle of Sauvignon Blanc at my friendly liquor store. Heading downtown, I cruised Main Street till it intersected with Armory, and took Armory to The Quay. More a cobblestoned walkway than a street, The Quay led downhill, wrapping around the perimeter of the harbor before dead-ending at an old dock with a big tug and some runabouts snugged against it. No house in sight. I got out of the car with the wine and tried the last building before the water, a supply shop called Joe's Marine. Murky fluorescents made the place look ghostly. The reversible sign, on a triangle of twine inside the glass door, said CLOSED. I stepped back to check the windows on the second floor. No lights on, but the reflection from a streetlight suggested the upper level was used by Joe for storage, not by Liz for residence. I could hear some music coming from the direction of the tug, and a lantern shimmered in its wheelhouse as the boat rode ugly over the chop of the waves. I decided it was time to ask for corrective directions.

The tug, pointing in toward land, looked brand-new. The hull appeared to be wooden, though, and I couldn't imagine they still made them that way. Stenciled along the bow was the word *Shepherd*. A metal gangplank successively barred by two tined gates spanned the water from dock to deck.

I said, "Ahoy the *Shepherd!* Anyone aboard?"

A small black door at deck level opened, and Liz Rendall came out with a spatula in her hand and a short apron over even shorter shorts. "Welcome to paradise. Surprised?"

I moved my eyes from stem to stern. "A little."

She reached back inside the door with her free hand, and a grating sound rose from the locks on the gates. "All the modern conveniences. Come aboard."

Pushing through the gates, I was struck by how heavy the second one was. "Who was your security consultant?"

Liz cocked her head at me.

I said, "This second gate. Electrified, right?"

She nodded slowly. "They said you were good."

"Who did?"

"The people I called about you. Let me just turn down dinner and then I'll give you the tour. Come in."

I gave her the wine, accepted her compliment on it, and took in the galley as she iced the bottle. Jenn-Air double stove, butcher-block counters and preparation island, all copper pots and pans. *"Better Homes and Gardens* been by yet?"

"Let me show you the rest of it."

I followed as Rendall moved aft through an opening that seemed about twice as wide as a working tug would have. "This is the dining room."

The table was Danish modern, four chairs around it. She continued to a balustrade. "And this is the living room."

I joined her at the rail and looked down a full set of steps into a cavernous space. Elaborately casual sectional furniture, complemented by some rattan chairs and matching tables. Stereo and television consoles mounted in recesses at just above head height from the floor. Or hull. On the opposite wall, a half-staircase led up to a door. Draped between the portholes were tapestries whose country of origin I couldn't even guess.

I said, "Liz, this is spectacular."

She beamed. "It wasn't as hard as it might look. I bought this beauty from an offshore oil company for four thousand bucks when she couldn't pass inspection anymore." Liz moved her hand in an arc. "They'd already lifted the deck and pulled the twin diesels. I had my people remove the old boilers and put in a 3,500-watt generator. Joe—he's the guy who owns the marine shop at the end of the dock—Joe and the utilities let me tie into his lines, so I really don't need the generator except as a fail-safe."

"Must have cost a fortune."

"Not as much as a studio condo in Boston. Since the basic structure was only four, the rest came in under a hundred thousand."

"That's still pretty steep for a reporter."

"I was married once. He was close to rich. When we got divorced, the property settlement was enough for this, the Alfa, and a sixteen-footer lashed down the dock aways."

"Those other stairs lead to the porch?"

"Yes, but let's go out and around."

Rendall retraced her steps back through the dining room and galley, then outside and around to the ten-by-fifteen porch, facing southwest toward the ocean. "This space used to be a chart room, but I wanted a screened area for enjoying the sea breeze at night. Plus with the sun deck beyond it to the stern, I can sit outside so long as the bugs cooperate."

"Looks like you've got everything."

"Gets better. Come on."

There was an outside gangway on the port side of the porch. Resting on two hooks drilled into the wood was a spear gun. A nasty metal arrow about eighteen inches long already was lodged in the channel on top of the tube.

I said, "The weaponry original equipment?"

She laughed. "Ever live on a boat?"

"No."

"What's the biggest rat you've ever seen?"

"I think I get the point."

Liz took the gun from the wall, playfully stretching one of two, thick rubber bands near a notch on the shaft itself. "I'm allergic to cat fur, and a bullet would do as much damage to the boat as to the rat. With this thing, the shaft goes through and sticks the little pest to the wall or deck. That still keeps him at arm's length from me as I scrape him off on a cleat and into the water for the crabs."

"Lovely. The other rubber band makes it two-barreled?"

"What . . . oh, no. See this second notch on the shaft? If I nock both slings and pull the trigger, I get twice the power, but I'd never get the damn shaft back out of the wood."

I told her I was ready for the rest of the tour, and she put the spear gun back on the hooks.

At the top of the gangway was another, smaller sun deck, with lounge chair and metal table. "I come up here when I want to tan all over." She smiled saucily.

"This the wheelhouse?"

"Yes." Rendall opened a small door by turning a brass ring to undo the latch.

Inside, her bedroom stretched to the curved glass-front parlor from which the helmsman would guide a working tug. "I had them extend the wheelhouse aft, even though it meant cutting down the smokestack. I didn't have much choice about that, though, unless I wanted a bedroom the size of a walk-in closet. This way, I can have a full bath up here as well as downstairs forward of the galley."

She'd kept most of the wood and metal, even the wheel itself and the handled ratcheting device that instructed the engine room on speed and direction. The bed was queen-sized and built with its headboard into the wall.

"Everything but a two-car garage."

Liz sat back onto the bed. "I even have that. My deal with Joe includes renting out a garage behind his store. Nasharbor isn't in Boston's league as far as stolen cars are concerned, but there's no sense in tempting anybody with the Alfa. This way, you can't see it from the street."

I nodded. She drew her right leg languorously across the comforter till it tucked under the left one.

"In fact, you can't see much of anything from the street. That's why I can go out on the upper deck in the altogether."

"And tease the sea gulls."

"Among other visitors."

I crossed my arms and leaned against the doorjamb. "Who'd you call about me?"

"Who'd I? . . ."

"Call. You said you checked me out."

"Oh, nobody in particular. I just thought as Jane's executrix, I ought to find out a little about you."

"Like what?"

"Like you haven't had the easiest time of it. You lost your wife young, you hit the booze but you're not a drunk." The saucy smile again. "Like you're technically available but you're dating some lawyer."

"You're being straight with me, let me be straight with you. Six months ago, you might have been the one. You look enough like my wife to be a sister. But the lawyer's the one for me now, so why don't we just have a nice professional dinner?"

"Meaning you're not married, but you might as well be."

"Like that."

Liz stood up and leaned in close, just brushing my neck with her lips. "Minds were meant to be changed."

* * *

"The stuffing?"

"Portuguese-style French bread for the base, minced lobster, a little dill. It's not hard."

"It's great with the cod."

Liz put down her fork and sipped the wine. "So is this. The lawyer teach you?"

"No. My wife liked wine and learned about it. She taught me enough to know what I enjoy and what to look for."

"My ex never taught me anything, except how to cash an alimony check."

"You married long?"

"Three years. Seemed like three hundred. We lived in New York. He was a stockbroker, fifteen years older. It was fine at first, lots of parties and yachts and things. Mostly just things, though, acquisition of assets. You know what I mean?"

"He bought things for investment, not enjoyment?"

"Exactly. That's exactly what he did. I was like that to him. An athletic young wife who would mature well, paying many dividends in the form of rousing sex and admiring glances at the club."

"Sounds kind of unfulfilling for you."

"'Unfulfilling.' How diplomatic. He was a domineering shit, is what he was. But that was okay, in a sense. I left a crummy job at a crummy paper to marry him, and I'm glad I got life in the fast lane out of my system."

"What led you to come up here?"

Rendall poured herself a little more wine. "I went to college in Boston. Simmons."

"Fine school."

"Yeah. It was a good time to be in college, too. Cambodia semester my sophomore year. You remember that?"

"I was a little older."

She smiled. " 'You carry the years lightly.' "

"Is that a quote?"

"I think so, but I have trouble remembering things like that. You . . . you went to Vietnam, right?"

"Your sources are still batting a thousand."

"I . . . I don't want to pry or anything, but I'm thinking of doing a series for the paper on vets today, not just the crack-ups, but a cross section. Could I call you about it?"

I reached for the bottle. "Okay if I say no?"

"Sure, sure."

There was an awkward silence. I said, "So why Nasharbor?"

"Huh?"

"Simmons explains your coming back this way, but why Nasharbor in particular?"

"Oh, that's easy. After the divorce, I needed a change of scenery. I'd had it with the City. New York was becoming what it wasn't. I wanted to leave before I became what it is now."

"Which is?"

"All hype and money. I know that sounds pretty clichéd, but I really could see it in just the four years I put in down there. Everybody was into things they couldn't afford."

I swung my head around the boat. "This isn't what I'd call the brink of survival."

Liz shook her head. "No, no. I didn't think you understood me. I don't mean they couldn't afford things in the cash-and-carry sense. It was more that everybody was trying to be something they weren't, hyping the person next to them in every encounter. No straight talk, no real people."

"And Nasharbor's real."

"You bet it is." She got a look in her eye, a lot like Bruce Fetch extolling redevelopment. "Here we've got every problem and every advantage that real people do. The old, the sick, the poor. The ones trying to help them or exploit them. People care about the real lives they lead, not some image of life they lifted from TV. It's like the difference between a movie made in the forties and one made today, you know?"

"James Stewart and June Allyson are real, Sean Penn and Madonna aren't."

She pouted. "You're making fun of me, aren't you?"

"Almost, but not quite. Sorry."

"You're forgiven. Help me clear the table?"

We shuttled the dirty dishes to the galley. Liz piled them into a dishwasher and said, "You ready for dessert, or would you rather wait?"

"How about if you show me what you found at the paper first?"

"Sure. Here . . ." She reached into a cabinet, came out with some Bénédictine and Brandy. "Take the B & B and two glasses down into the living room. I've got the file in my study."

I carried the bottle and the small bell glasses down the stairs, setting them on the coffee table and myself on a rattan chair. I rocked back, finding it a little tippy. Liz appeared shortly, untying the string on an accordion file and withdrawing a sheaf of newspapers and a reporter's spiral notebook. "It looks like more than it is, I'm afraid."

She sat on a sectional piece next to me. "Why don't you just follow along on the notes from the police incident, then you can read Jane's articles on Coyne and Dykestra while I get dessert?"

"Okay."

Rendall started through the notebook, stopped,

then turned one more sheet. "Here we go." She ran her finger down the page. "Date of death: July 12, 1971. A little farther back than you thought. Decedent's name: Meller, Dwight. Age: eighteen."

"Who was the reporter?"

"C. E. Griffin."

"You know this Griffin?"

"Never heard the name before. Definitely not there now, though."

"How about the paper's employment records?"

"I checked. State law says we only have to keep personnel records a year, but we keep them three. Even so, no mention of a Griffin. I talked to some people in the backshop and pressmen from that era. Nobody remembers him. Or her. From the way the story read, though, I can make a guess."

"Which is?"

"An intern."

"You mean a student?"

"Right. Usually a journalism major, working for the summer. The prose was awkward, redundant. Like an editor under deadline throttled it to make the piece presentable."

"Go on."

"I didn't copy it word for word, but apparently Hagan and Schonsy interrupted the Meller boy in the course of a burglary. They chased Meller, caught him, then Meller got in a lucky punch with a brick, resulting in Hagan having to restrain the boy, who died of a broken neck."

Sounded just like Schonstein's story. "Any other witnesses?"

"Just the reporter."

"Griffin?"

"Yes. I copied that . . . yeah, here it is. 'This reporter saw the altercation from the mouth of the alley, corroborating the police version of the event.'"

Schonstein had omitted the reporter. "Read me that again."

She did. I said, "Would the paper let a reporter write a story when the reporter was involved in it?"

"Are you kidding? A killing, even an accidental one, is page-one stuff in a town this size. I'd have whip-sawed Arbuckle into letting me write it under byline or tell him he could read my story in the *Boston Herald*."

"I know somebody at the *Herald*. Would it be worth my while to have him check their morgue on this?"

Rendall thought about it, riffling two more pages. "I doubt it. Looks like the *Beacon* ran only one more piece, when Hagan and Schonsy were officially exonerated. And that was only a page-three item because of two fires and a boat being lost in a storm."

"How about photos?"

"First article had one of the alley, one of Schonstein with blood on him at the hospital, Hagan kind of holding him up. Looked like the Meller boy really nailed him with the brick, by the way. Couple of sentences of bio on the cops, how both were local products, married with kids, that kind of thing."

"This Meller have any family?"

"The piece mentioned a mother, but didn't give an address, just 'of this city.' I tried the telephone directories at the paper, even the old ones we keep, but came up empty."

"Anything about the Meller boy's employment, education?"

"Unemployed dropout. Sounded like a loner, too. No friends mentioned."

"Anything else in the article?"

Liz skipped back and forth through the notebook a few times. "Sorry. After the big splash, even the paper treated it as pretty much cut-and-dried."

"How about the recent stuff on Coyne and Dykestra?"

"Here and . . . here. The redevelopment ones are a lot more elaborate. They're in reverse chronological order." She stood. "We've got cherry pie, fresh baked, with vanilla or coconut almond ice cream."

"Coconut almond?"

"So I splurged a little. I thought I was gonna get lucky, remember?"

As I watched her climb the stairs, my mind strayed to how close we could have come, six months ago. "I'll go with vanilla."

"I figured you would."

The pieces on Coyne were pretty cryptic, probably more an indication of Arbuckle's judgment than Jane's passion. The dragnet article named Coyne as one person arrested. The stabbing article mentioned a derelict witness, but no more detail than Hagan and Vip already had told me.

There were three redevelopment stories in all. Jane's first one dealt with the concept as applied to Nasharbor in general, mentioning Richard Dykestra only as a teaser toward the next two. The second story was specific and rough, how Dykestra's dream was being financed by We the People, chapter and verse. The third story contained some unresponsive observations by Little Richard, echoed, as I suspected they would be, by Bruce Fetch at the NRA. I could see Dykestra resenting Jane, but I didn't see anything she'd done beyond pasting together the effects of a dozen public documents and events.

Rendall descended the stairs balancing a tray that

made clinking noises with each step. I poured out some B & B for each of us, and we finished dessert before we resumed talking.

I said, "You find any notes on Coyne or the cops in Jane's desk at the *Beacon?*"

"No, nothing. Maybe at her apartment?"

"I checked when I saw Mrs. O'Day. Zero."

"Too bad." Liz gestured toward the redevelopment articles. "So, what'd you think?"

I told her.

Frowning, she said, "Granted it was all public information, but wouldn't you have been a little more than rankled at Jane for spreading it so thick?"

"I guess I just don't see it. So Dykestra got bailed out by the taxpayers. It all seems aboveboard, and nothing worse happened to him except maybe the pols won't be so quick to lend a hand next time."

"What if her next story went a little deeper than public knowledge?"

"How do you mean?"

"What if some of the numbers got a little cooked before Dykestra and Fetch served them up to the pols?"

"You have any proof of that?"

"No, but Jane was sure close to Fetch before Coyne and the porno craze overtook her. It wouldn't surprise me much if she learned some things from Bruce during pillow talk that she could have documented given enough time."

"Again, you have any proof?"

Rendall sighed. "No. I just can't see the Coyne thing being anybody's reason to kill her. And if it wasn't that, or the redevelopment project, I've got to believe she really did commit suicide. I just don't like that any better than murder, I guess."

"Maybe I should check Jane's house again."

"For notes and so on?"

"Yes."

"I can save you a trip. I have to go there again tomorrow."

"How come?"

"The funeral. I already picked a dress for the undertaker to . . . to use. But Jane's aunt's coming in from Kansas, and I promised I'd take her through the place."

"What time's the funeral?"

"Eleven-thirty. At Almeida's on Exeter Street. You coming?"

I wanted to say no outright, but instead I said, "Who else are you expecting?"

"Not many. I'm assuming at least some of my colleagues won't be too scandalized to attend."

"Because of the suicide atmosphere, you mean?"

"Yes and no. Suicide's the rationalization they'll use. The fact they just didn't like her much is the real reason they'll stay away." She drank some more. "Could we maybe talk about something else? I mean, you came here tonight to take my mind off the funeral, remember?"

"Sorry. Any other topic is fine. You first."

Liz mock-toasted by touching her glass to mine. "I like a man who doesn't drink coffee."

"Just never cared for the taste of it."

She swirled her liqueur. " 'Why drink the grindings of beans when nectar flows so freely?' "

"Another quote?"

"Yes, but I can attribute this one. Malcolm Peete, our resident lush."

"Just because a guy's a lush doesn't mean he's stupid."

"And just because he isn't stupid doesn't mean he does his job."

"When you replace Arbuckle, you going to do something about it?"

She inhaled the warm liquid. "Mal tell you to ask me that?"

"No."

Rendall poured another shot. "Peete thinks he's invulnerable. He's wrong. Arbuckle doesn't know how to manage the big boys, the executive editor and the publisher. It'd take me all of three months in Arbuckle's chair before I undermined all that old war-buddy stuff to the point that Peete would have to drive his drunken ass through the snows of another city. Believe it."

I did. "At least you could offer him transportation."

She looked at me quizzically. "Why?"

"He lost his license."

"Who told you that?"

"He did. Implicitly, anyway."

"No. No, that's wrong. I'd have heard about it. Besides, he's so tight with the cops he squeaks when he goes by one."

"Meaning he does drive?"

"Well, he's got a car, and I've seen it in our lot often enough the last few months. So unless he's hired a chauffeur, he's driving himself."

"What kind of car?"

"Old Volkswagen." Liz looked at me more shrewdly. "Does that make a difference somehow?"

I finished my drink. "I'll have to let you know. Mind if I use your phone?"

She pointed to a turquoise princess model on an end table. "I'll take these back up and give you some privacy."

"Thanks."

I dialed the motel and drew Jones on the third ring. "Crestview."

"Emil, John Cuddy."

"I got your goddam message you been so hot to get."

"What's it say?"

"Guy sounded like a boozer."

"He's a derelict, Emil."

"Well, whatever the hell he is, he's gonna be waiting for you."

"Tonight?"

"Hell, yes, tonight."

"Where?"

"In the alley behind your favorite establishment."

"Bun's?"

"That's what he said. You sure you bat from the right side of the plate, Cuddy?"

"He give you a time?"

"I asked him that. He said you were too goddam cheap to give him your watch, so you could just hope he'd still be there when you arrived. Goddam uppity bum."

"Thanks, Emil. Sorry to inconvenience you."

"I won't let it turn into a habit."

He hung up.

Liz leaned her elbows on the balustrade above me, shifting her weight from bent leg to bent leg, rolling her rump in a one-two rhythm. Probably an aerobics exercise.

She said, "Sounds like you're leaving me."

"Sorry. Thanks for dinner. It was terrific."

"So are the stars. Over the water you can see them real clear. Count them even." She accentuated one repetition of the exercise. "Especially good viewing from the wheelhouse."

Climbing the stairs, I drew even with her as she slid her arms up and around my neck.

I looked into her eyes. "If I were to say, 'Maybe next time,' I'd be lying."

She shook her head. "I know."

SEVENTEEN

The Strip had one strong point: parking never seemed to be a problem, even at ten-thirty on a Thursday night. Leaving the Prelude near Bun's, I entered the alley just as a cloud passed across the moon, followed by a flash of lightning and the eventual rumble of distant thunder. Liz would be missing her stars. A second flash allowed me to spot Vip, curled around the wheels of a dumpster maybe ten feet from the back door of Gotbaum's bar.

Bending down, I said, "You called me?"

His feet, shod in old combat boots, squirmed and resettled.

I tugged on one of the boots. "Vip, it's John Cuddy. You called me?"

Using an elbow as a fulcrum, he passed a palm over his face. "Awake, officer. I's awake."

"Vip, it's John Cuddy."

"Cuddy?"

"Yes. You called me, remember?"

"Right, right. You don't gots to spell it out for me, you know? I'm not a fuckin drunk, like some peoples I could mention."

"You ready to talk now?"

"You ready to pay now?"

I took a twenty from my pocket and held it close enough for him to see the denomination. "Start talking."

"Not till I gets the twenty."

"You said you trusted me because of how I handled those three teenagers, right? I give you the twenty first, and I don't like what I hear, I can just take it back. So why don't we exchange value like gentlemen here, okay?"

Vip grunted. "You wants it short or long?"

"Long would be nice."

He arranged himself into a sitting position, back against a bag of trash that hadn't quite made it into the dumpster. I found a beer case, stamped it flat, and lowered myself Indian-style.

"Shaping up to be a dry night, that one. Not much action, nobody gots no bottle. Gets me some supper up along the mission off Second, some kind of seafood shit gots more potatoes in it than anything, but what else be new under the sun? One of the boys say Charlie out and about, so I comes down here."

"Charlie Coyne?"

"'Course Charlie Coyne. Who the fuck you wanting to know about?"

"He's the one."

"Then hows about you shuts up and listens to what I gots to say about him?"

"Fine."

Vip seemed mollified. "Charlie, he a piece of work, that one. Gets hisself shit-faced over in the bar. Buys hisself some cheap shit offen the barkeep. Then come out here, pass it 'round to the boys."

"You talk with him that night?"

"Talk with Charlie? You gots to be shitten me, man. Charlie, he don't start coming out here till he so shit-faced, he lucky he still raise a hand for to drink with."

"What happened after he started passing the bottle around?"

"They's a fight over it, like they always is. Fuckin bums, they goes up the alley a piece, squabbling over the thing like hens over a new bandy-cock. I lets 'em go, ain't gots no time for fighting over things."

"Then what?"

Vip looked around melodramatically, a confidant in a silent movie. "Biggish dude kind of crawl over to Charlie. Never laid eyes on him before, and I been in this here alley mosta two years now. I figures maybe he gonna rip old Charlie off, buy his own bottle. Dude gets close onto Charlie, starts going through the pockets, you know? Not like a queer, more searching for something. Anyway, musta struck a sweet spot, 'cause old Charlie, he come 'round, shouting and cussing. Had us a moon that night, we surely did, and I sees the blade coming out and down, then they's rolling 'round, spitting and tussling, but that Charlie, he too drunk and shit, he too skinny anyway for to take the big man. I hears a noise I hears before, and I knows he's gone."

"What noise?"

Vip worked his mouth. "Noise a blade make going through the lung. You hears it oncst, you never forgets it later."

"Then what happened?"

"Big dude gets hisself up, don't really look 'round or nothing, just takes hisself off down the alley here, hopping on one leg and dragging the tuther. I sees this knife sticking out the side of it. Don't seem right."

"What didn't seem right?"

"The knife. You ever sees a man stuck like that?"

"Slashed or stuck in the guts, yeah. Not in the leg."

"Well then, you gots some to learn, you does. Man stuck like that big one, he gonna pull that sucker out afore he does no jogging, get me?"

"I get you."

Vip shook his head. "No, don't seem right."

Another bolt of lightning, a clap of thunder on its tail this time. "You said the moon was up that night. You get a look at the big guy's face?"

"Some. Like I says afore, never did see him 'round."

"Can you describe him?"

"White man, gots a watch cap pulled down over his ears."

I thought about my scrape with the Buick. "Watch cap?"

"Yeah. Fuckin cold in these alleys of a night, you don't gots something on your head. Shit, man, here she come."

I felt a few raindrops, too. Vip started what promised to be a two-minute program of getting to his feet.

I said, "You tell the cops all this?"

"Yeah, yeah. I tells the same things, they writes 'em down, grins on their fuckin faces, like they don't gots to believe a word I say."

"They take you to the station, show you mug shots?"

"You gotta be shitting me, man. They's the cops,

194

they's seen it all afore. Bum gots knife, bum wants bottle, bum kills bum. End of story."

The drizzle gave way to real rain as Vip finally made it to his feet and took a few hesitant steps.

"Shit, man. Gives me my twenty, huh? I don't wanna catch no 'monia outta this here."

I gave him the twenty. He squirreled it inside his coat and past three or four layers, making faces until he reached deep enough to feel secure. He set off down the alley, lurching like a newborn colt.

I said, "Vip, you call me again, alright? Let me know you're okay?"

He started what might have been a wave, but began to sing instead.

EIGHTEEN

◆

The storm woke me twice during the night, but Friday dawned cloudless, the rain living on only through isolated pools and wet grass. I had an Egg McMuffin and three containers of orange juice at the Golden Arches, then drove to police headquarters. I had to wait only five minutes before the desk sergeant sent me up to see Hagan.

Reading a duty roster, Hagan wore a short-sleeved dress shirt and knit tie, the hair on his forearms sandy and thick. "What is it this time, Cuddy?"

"I had a talk with your star witness last night."

"What witness?"

"The derelict who saw Charlie Coyne get stabbed."

"Great. Appreciate the follow-up. Anything else?"

"He says the killer stood up and hopped away on a bad leg."

"Your leg has a tendency to go bad, you get a knife jammed into it."

"Or if you have some preexisting injury."

"Meaning?"

"Meaning it seems just a little odd that a guy with a knife in his leg is going to run away on it without taking the knife out first."

"So?"

"So I'm thinking, what if the knife in the leg is a mask for a limp the killer had before he went after Charlie."

Hagan leaned back into the chair, blowing out a breath. "Your bum see Coyne's killer walking okay before the fight?"

"No. Never saw him before and never saw him walk. Said the killer crawled over to Charlie."

"Doesn't fly. Too complicated. Besides, Coyne was known to carry a knife, and the responding unit didn't find one at the scene."

"Which makes the knife in the leg the one Coyne carried."

"Right."

I said, "That assumes the killer brought a knife to use on Coyne. The witness says the guy searched Coyne before fighting with him. Suppose the killer was looking for Coyne's own knife, stabbed him with it, then just stuck the knife through a pad or something strapped to the leg, to make it look like Coyne had gotten him so as to cover the limp the killer had coming into the fight."

Hagan chewed the inside of his cheek, then shook his head. "You're going on an assumption, too. You're assuming the killer's also the one who did your client, right?"

"It would make sense."

"But it doesn't."

"How come?"

"Basic principle of homicide. Rust died by overdose, Coyne by violence, specifically a knife. Different methods entirely. A professional finds a way to kill, he stays with it because it works and he doesn't get caught doing it. A nut, he finds a way he likes, he stays with that because he's got to, the voice of his dead mother or whatever tells him to keep using it. The same person wouldn't do Coyne one way, then Rust another. Variety isn't his spice of life."

"How about an amateur?"

Hagan said, "Amateur?"

"Yeah. You said a pro and a nutcase would both stay consistent. How about an amateur?"

"You figure Rust asked a bum in for hot cocoa Monday night?"

"I figure maybe the big guy who did Coyne wasn't a bum, remember? Also, if he knew killers stay consistent, what better way to disguise the crimes being related?"

Hagan came forward in his chair. "I don't see it that way, Cuddy."

"Which way do you see it?"

"The way it happened. Shitbird gets knifed, depressed girl feels responsible and decides to chugalug her life."

"I want to talk to the mother of Dwight Meller."

Hagan's face drained like somebody pulled a plug in his throat. "Why?"

"If you're being straight with me, it seems you'd tell me where I can find her. She's not listed in the book, seems like she never has been."

His Adam's apple rode up and down. "You ever kill anybody, Cuddy?"

"Yes."

"Intentionally?"

"Yes."

"How many?"

"All of them."

"Well, I haven't. Not ever, not once. The knee kept me out of the draft. I used to think it was a miracle the force would have me. Then came that night. Aside from the Meller boy, I never took a life. And Meller was unintentional. I killed him alright, but I never meant to."

I said, very quietly, "I'd still like to talk to his mother. You want me to waste a day checking welfare, water bills. . . ."

Hagan blinked, then blinked again, but I think more at what was inside his head than at me. "Costigan Street, over on the north side. Number 57."

"All these years, and you still remember the address."

"Ought to. After that night, I drove by it every day for a month, trying to get up the courage to tell his mother I was sorry. Now get out."

I was reaching for the knob when the door opened and a youngish plainclothes cop stuck his head in. "Sorry, Captain, but you said you wanted to know when we got an ID on the swimmer in the alley."

"Go ahead. Mr. Cuddy was just leaving."

As the cop passed me, he said to Hagan, "Manos made him. Only had a nickname. 'Vip.'"

I closed my eyes and turned back around as Hagan said, "Vip?"

I said, "It stood for 'Very Important Person.' Your star witness."

Hagan clenched his teeth. "Coincidence, Cuddy."

I shouted, "Oh, for crissake!"

Hagan rose from his seat and pounded a fist on his desk. The paperwork and the young cop jumped about the same height. "The guy was a bum! They found him with an empty quart of rye still in his hand, facedown in the rain puddle. They get so soused, they can't even tell they're drowning."

"I was with the guy last night, Captain, remember? It was ten-thirty, maybe eleven. He didn't have a bottle on him, and your liquor stores would all be closed by then."

Hagan really erupted. "You gave him some money, didn't you?"

I didn't reply.

"You gave him money so he'd talk to you, and he took it to some blind pig. You think a bum doesn't know where to buy a bottle after-hours?"

I didn't want to hear the rest of it, but I'd pushed Meller down Hagan's throat, and he had a right to do the same to me.

"They sell him the rye, Cuddy, and he downs it, then goes belly-whopping in three inches of water. What the fuck did you think he was gonna do with your money, Saint John? Buy himself some new threads, maybe a dry bed for the night? You fuckin sanctimonious asshole, you said you never killed anybody without meaning to? Well, stand proud, brother. You just got credited with your first."

I'd heard enough and left, the young cop's mouth set for catching flies.

If I had my bearings right, the button I was pushing belonged to 57 Costigan Street, but I couldn't hear any chimes responding inside. I tried knocking; no one answered. Then I heard a vaguely familiar sound that I couldn't immediately place. A whispery, intermittent ticking noise, like someone repeatedly thumbing along and through fifty pages of a book. It was coming from behind the house.

Moving to the side yard, I noticed how similar the house was to Gail Fearey's, the major difference being the condition of each. The exterior paint here was pale peach and appeared, if not fresh, at least not completely abandoned. Mrs. Meller maintained ivy and other vines along the sunny wall, with flowers planted in a pleasing pattern beneath them.

As I turned the back corner, I could see an older, slight woman pushing a prehistoric hand mower, the thresher blades making that ticking sound. The yard was only about forty by fifty, which made the manual method seem quite rational. Her back to me, she advanced, retreated, and drove on, two or three feet at a time, waltzing to a silent tune.

I said, "Mrs. Meller?"

She quartered her progress, but only to cover a patch extending into a bed of violets. I crossed the yard, repeating her name. I was only a few steps from her when she spun around, a frightened look in her eyes.

I quickly said, "I'm sorry, I didn't mean—"

She held up her right hand in a stop sign, which had the desired effect on me. She cupped the hand to her ear, then two fingers to her lips in a shush gesture. Then she shook her head.

Deaf, and mute. Approaching sixty, her face tapered to a delicate chin and was framed by graying hair in what used to be called a pixie cut.

Mouthing the words in an exaggerated way, I said, "Do you read lips?"

She held up her hand again, this time thumb and index finger an inch apart.

"A little?"

Mrs. Meller nodded.

I produced my identification. She read it, looked up at me.

"Jane Rust hired me before she died."

Mrs. Meller seemed baffled.

"You didn't know her?"

Negative shake.

"I think her death might have something to do with the death of your son, Dwight."

She crossed her arms and dropped her gaze. Gulping once hard, the woman made up her mind. She moved toward the back door, indicating I should follow.

The inside of the house was as perfectly arranged and kept as the landscaping. We sat on a couch in her living room, she pointing first to a red bulb in a fixture mounted on the opposite wall. Pressing her thumb on an imaginary button in the air in front of her, she pointed next to a lamp, then opened and closed her fist like someone signaling "five" over and over.

"When the doorbell is pushed, the red light flashes?"

She nodded, smiling. Then her expression shifted. From the drawer in the end table she produced a large manila tablet like elementary school kids used when learning the alphabet. Mrs. Meller wrote quickly in capital letters, her syntax jumbled.

"WHAT YOU WANT KNOW ME"

Indicating the pad and then myself, I said, "Should I write my questions down for you?"

She shook her head, gesturing toward me and my mouth, then her and the pad. I got it.

As she stared intently at my lips, I said, "I know how the police said the incident happened. Do you believe them?"

"DWIGHT AND ME POOR BUT HIM THIEF NO"

"What do you think happened?"

"POLICE LIE ME NO KNOW WHY"

"Had Dwight ever been in trouble with the authorities before?"

As I spoke the word *authorities* her eyes fluttered, confused.

I said, "Trouble with the police before that night?"

Shaking again, she wrote, "KIDS SCHOOL MAKE FUN ME DWIGHT MANY FIGHT"

"Aside from fights at school, though, any . . . any crimes?"

Dogmatically no.

"What would he have been doing in that alley?"

She seemed to bite back a memory. Then, "DWIGHT DEAF BUT TALK SOME THEN KIDS MAKE FUN GIRLS MAKE FUN"

Mrs. Meller looked up at me, but I didn't understand, and she could see it before I could say it.

"DWIGHT GO THE STRIP FOR GIRLS"

I paused, embarrassed for her and myself and for a boy I'd never met. His visits to The Strip weren't varsity larks.

"The newspapers had only a couple of stories about what happened. Did you ever have anyone look into it, like a lawyer, maybe?"

"NO MONEY JUST ME"

"You looked into it?"

She seemed hurt, and I realized how my doubt must have appeared to her.

She wrote, "BOOK YOU WAIT" and left the room.

I folded my hands and tried to think of a way to apologize but couldn't.

Mrs. Meller returned with a scrapbook. Resuming her seat, she opened it on her lap.

The first few plastic sleeves held old photos, black-and-white and too small or too large for today's 35-millimeter standard. She reviewed them quickly, lingering on only two shots: a much younger she and a baby, followed by a noticeably younger she and a gawky fifteen-year-old boy. She glanced at me from the corner of an eye and proceeded until the photos were succeeded by newspaper clippings.

Mrs. Meller yielded the page turning to me. She had them all. The *Globe* and the *Herald* (still the *Herald Traveler* in those days) carried only the short pieces Liz Rendall had predicted. A candid photo of the young Hagan was attached to the *Herald* story, a police academy portrait of Hagan in a parade cap in the *Globe.* I skimmed the articles from the *Beacon,* which paralleled the content and style of what Liz had told me, down to the "C. E. Griffin" bylines.

Mrs. Meller had a *Beacon* picture Liz hadn't mentioned: Hagan and Schonstein, the latter barely recognizable through the Crusader's cross of bandages taped over his face. They were entering some sort of public building. The clipping was yellowed and the photo itself expectedly grainy.

There were eight more clippings in the book. One dealt with the clearing of the officers for their actions that night, and a second was Dwight Meller's awkwardly brief obituary. The final six chronicled Hagan's sequential promotions, with an Op-Ed piece broadly suggesting that he was the right man to next occupy the chair of chief.

I checked to make sure there were no more entries. I realized Mrs. Meller was watching me expectantly.

My demeanor must have conveyed the unspoken question "Is this it?," because she closed the book very carefully and formed her hands around the edges, straightening the leaves in a way I couldn't appreciate or caressing the memories in a way I could.

I started to say, "Mrs. Meller . . . ," but realized she wasn't looking at me. I touched her sleeve, and she tore herself from the past.

"Mrs. Meller, thank you for showing me this. I lost my wife before her time, and I know that going through all this again wasn't easy for you."

She reached for the tablet. "POLICE KILL DWIGHT YOU FIND OUT WHY TELL ME"

I said I'd try.

Wonder of wonders, Richard Dykestra was in his office. Even the receptionist seemed surprised.

Dykestra came through an inner door when he heard my voice. He said "Hold my calls" to her and "C'mon" to me.

A scale model of Harborside haunted a table near his desk. Pink telephone message slips were clustered next to a multilined Rolm receiver. I sat on a black leather hammock stitched to a chrome frame. Dykestra plopped into a big swivel chair, his feet resting pigeon-toed on the base of the chair.

"Thought me and you had our talk already."

"Some things came up. I remembered you saying Jane Rust never bought your explanations. Figured I'd give you the chance to sell them to me."

"Let's hear your questions."

"I read Jane's articles on redevelopment in general and you in particular."

"So?"

"So how'd she miss your settlement with Schonsy on the fire?"

I wanted to say it like that, watch for his reaction. He was as animated as a freeze-frame.

"I don't see what a cop's fall has to do with any of this here."

"You don't."

"No," said Dykestra. "He's an old guy, carrying this young kid down some stairs. He don't watch where he's going."

"Through the smoke, you mean?"

"Through whatever the fuck was going on that night."

"Yet you settled with him."

"Yeah. Yeah, I settled it."

"Insurance company involved?"

"You kidding? You know what they want for insurance on them four-deckers? They're wood. Fifty, sixty years old. Cost more in premiums than I gross in rents."

"Then where's the pressure to settle? Why not let him sue you, drag it out a few years before you've got to write the check?"

Dykestra shrugged. "Guy's a cop. A fuckin hero for saving the kid and everybody else in the building. Good public relations."

"No, Richie. Good private relations."

"I don't get you."

"Schonsy seems the kind of guy you don't short-change."

"Look, I got one of the Porto's lives in the place willing to say her uncle smokes in bed, okay? That means the fire's not my fault. But I got no insurance, no guarantee a jury with half of them Portos and the other half smokers are gonna see it that way. Plus, Schonsy was saying he tripped on the carpet coming down, and the staircase got so fuckin wrecked from the fire, who could say?"

"You have the building's title in a real estate trust?"

The face narrowed. "Yeah."

"Any other property in the same trust?"

"What's it to you?"

"I'm still wondering why you settled without a suit being filed. Even conceding you'd lose on the merits, why not just let Schonstein and his lawyer take the destroyed house and the land under it for what it's worth, so long as the trust didn't own any other parcels worth your saving?"

Dykestra's eyes made a circuit of the room. "Awright, you wanna know, I'll tell you so's you'll know. Cop like Schonsy, he's been around forever. He's got things on everybody. He makes a phone call here, drops a hint there, he could get everybody and his brother on my back. Everywhere I got property in the city. I don't need that, Jack. I don't need fines up the wazoo because my drunk fuck janitor in a twelve-unit complex ain't wearing a surgical mask when he takes the garbage cans to the curb."

"Not to mention fire inspections, building code violations—"

"You got the picture. Any more questions?"

"Yeah. How much was the settlement?"

"That you don't need to know." He picked up a message slip and pushed a button on the telephone console. "Give my regards to Boston, huh?"

"Maybe I'm not leaving town just yet."

"You ought to. I don't think Nasharbor's agreeing with you too good, you know?"

NINETEEN

◆

The Almeida Funeral Home was just off Main Street in a sprawling Victorian painted the obligatory white with black shutters. Three men with olive complexions were standing around a hearse and a limo in the driveway. The middle-aged one was shifting from foot to foot, a Clydesdale waiting professionally for the start of another parade. The two younger ones shared a cigarette and quiet jokes.

Inside, several viewing rooms branched off from the main foyer and central staircase. Next to one double doorway, a black felt board spelled in white plastic letters JANE RUST/PARLOR A. Managing editor Arbuckle was standing beside a seemingly sober Malcolm Peete. Each was talking out of the side of his mouth, as though that showed more respect for the deceased in the closed coffin. Kneeling at the casket was Bruce

Fetch, secretary Grace seated nearby. A dozen or so people milled around, a few of them faces I remembered from the city room. As a portly man moved aside, I could see Liz Rendall speaking with an elderly woman I recognized from one photo back on Jane's dresser. She wore a faded print dress that appeared ten years out of fashion. When Liz spotted me, she excused herself and came over.

Her eyes shone brightly over a face set in an appropriately subdued smile. "John, I'm glad you could make it."

I checked my watch. "I miss the services?"

"No. Jane wasn't religious, so I didn't think a service would be in keeping, especially given . . . the way she died. Almeida does a nice, simple job, regardless of, I think he said, 'the faith of the departed.'"

A silver-haired man in a morning coat with the manner of a patrician came into the room. He briefly took the elderly woman's hands in both of his and bowed slightly at the waist.

I said to Liz, "Almeida?"

"Yes."

"And Jane's aunt?"

"Uh-huh."

"You think I could ask her a few questions?"

Rendall frowned. "I don't know. She's been pretty good so far, but Jane was her only living relative, and I'm not sure how close she is to losing it."

"I'll tread softly."

Liz was cut off by Almeida saying, "May I have your attention, please?"

Everyone acceded, and Almeida explained the vehicular order of march. I noticed a few of the newspaper people growing sullen. Probably planned to stay only for the expected service in the funeral home, but now felt trapped into driving to the cemetery as well.

As Almeida concluded, I could see the aunt's eyes searching the room for Liz. Making contact, she approached us.

I quickly said to Liz, "Be easier for you if I rode in the limo, too?"

Before she could reply, the aunt was upon us, saying, "Liz, who is this good-looking young man? Your beau?"

Rendall said, "I wish, Ida. This is John Cuddy."

The aunt pressed my hand and said, "You were a friend of Janey's?"

I wasn't sure how much detail Liz had told her. "Yes, but only recently."

"Too bad. More friends like you and Liz, and I'll bet matters wouldn't have come to this." She noticed the room emptying out, and said, "If you don't have a ride to the cemetery, how about sharing the limousine with us?"

"Sure."

Ida gazed back at the casket. Almeida and the three I'd seen outside were politely waiting till the room was cleared before trundling the coffin out to the hearse.

Ida said, "Well, best be on our way, I guess. Leastways Jane's gotten a nice day. She would have liked that."

"Manhattan, Kansas. Ever hear of it?"

"No, ma'am. I haven't."

"Call ourselves 'The Little Apple.' Get it?"

"Yes, ma'am. Clever play on words."

"I think so. I do. Even got some decals and bumper stickers, that sort of thing. Couple of the shopkeepers made themselves a bundle on them. A bundle, word has it."

Liz and I sat next to each other in the limo, facing Ida in the most comfortable seat. I was thinking that if Ida was close to cracking, I'd hate to see her party mood.

"'Course it's still just a little town, just the university to keep it going, truth be told. But I've lived there all my life and never wanted anything else. Not like Janey, no."

"Did she stay in touch?"

"Oh, some. She'd write me, call on birthdays, Christmastime, that sort of thing. Janey was my sister's child, my younger sister. Died young, too. Right around Janey's age. Bad luck or bad seed."

"Janey talk much about what she was doing here?"

"On the newspaper?"

"Yes."

"No, not since she wrote me with her new address and all. Said she was real happy with it, her first 'real' job, she said. I guess the other papers didn't treat her so well, but if it wasn't for them, she wouldn't have been here, so who can say?"

"What do you mean?"

"Well, if it wasn't for her friend down in Florida, she wouldn't have gotten this job, but who can say whether it was good or ill, seeing as how things worked out for her."

Liz and I exchanged glances. "What friend?"

"Well, young man, I don't rightly know. Can't say she ever said, and if she did, I don't remember. Think it was just somebody from Florida who helped her, from the paper she worked on down there."

"Do you remember which paper?"

"Oh, mercy, no. She worked on so many, and they all sound the same to me, like nobody who ever owned them had as much imagination as a farmer naming his herd. But it was in Florida, for certain, near where she went to school."

I said to Liz, "You know where that was?"

"Probably Miami. They've got—"

"No, no. Wasn't Miami. Miami I would have remembered. Ry Bicks, he moved down there when his wife took sick. Couldn't ever understand Ry's doing that, never even saw the place before he upped and took her there, but I would have remembered Miami. When I read Janey's letter, I mean."

I said, "Tampa, Gainesville, Talla—"

"Gainesville! Gainesville, yes, I remember wondering if that's where the dog food came from, you know? Yes, it was Gainesville alright, whatever their newspaper is."

I was about to ask something when the driver slewed to the right and through the cemetery gate. As he proceeded slowly down the macadam, Ida looked around and her lower lip began to quiver.

She said, "Trees. Oh my, that's nice. Janey would have liked having trees around her."

Liz shot me a look that said, "Enough, okay?," and I had to agree with her.

Almeida was as short and sweet over the grave as he had been indoors. I could appreciate the heavily Catholic parts of the ceremony that he necessarily, but smoothly, deleted. The dozen or so mourners stood uncomfortably close together, Fetch directly behind me, Grace next to him.

Ida, weakening slowly, was between Liz and me. Liz

had her right arm around the aunt's waist for support. Ida reached down with her right hand and clasped my left in that bony, intense way older people have. She cried softly into a hankie. The hankie gave off a faint scent of lilac.

Almeida, from the tone of his voice, was approaching the last few sentences when I felt Liz tug on my suit pocket with the hand behind Ida's back. I ignored it, but she tugged harder.

I looked first at Liz, then at what had drawn her attention. Coming across the grounds, perhaps forty yards away, was Gail Fearey, carrying her diapered son curled in a skinny arm. Fearey was running, a desperate, knock-kneed caricature of a punt-returner whose team is losing in the fourth quarter.

Liz immediately hunched closer to Ida, getting a better grip. I moved around the grave as Almeida turned to see what the now-audible running was all about.

Before I could get between Fearey and the grave, she started screaming, "Biiiiiitch! Murdering fuckin biiiiitch!"

Tiger, who had been quiet till now, began to wail. I said, "Gail, please . . ." and took her free arm gently.

She wrestled away from me with surprising strength. Tearing off the child's soiled diaper, Fearey flung the cloth onto the coffin itself.

"You biiiitch! You fuckin biiiitch! The only fuckin thing I had, and you killed him! You fuckin biiiitch!"

Almeida's people moved with calm precision toward Gail. She felt the human net closing and whirled around, running back the way she came. When we didn't pursue her, she stopped. Bending over at the ground, Fearey screamed, "biiiitch!" The baby's weight nearly toppled her as she seemed to throw up. It was then run/stop/scream/heave at roughly ten-yard intervals until she ascended a low hill and disappeared from sight.

I heard Peete's voice say, "Christ, I need a drink."

TWENTY

"The real shame of it all is the absence of creativity, don't you think?"

"How do you mean?" I said.

"Well, consider it, good sir. 'The Almeida Funeral Home.' It's flat, unappealing. Would you want to be buried from there?"

I'd had enough vodka to think about it. Malcolm Peete used the gap to pour another triple into his glass. We'd both wanted a postmortem after Gail Fearey's scene at the grave, and Peete even asked Liz Rendall and Arbuckle to join us. Liz begged off on the ground that she thought she should look after Ida. Arbuckle just begged off.

"No."

Peete looked up from the bottle. "What's that?"

"I said no, I wouldn't want to be buried from there."

"Of course you wouldn't. Nobody would. Then again, by the time you have need of such services, the option is no longer yours. That's why Madison Avenue has to step in. A niche needs filling."

"Don't get you."

He set down his glass, spreading his hands. "Look, currently the choice of home is made by the survivors, correct?"

"Correct."

"Well, that's the problem. The survivors can't very well be clever and buoyant about it. They have to show some respect for the deceased, as a result of which the mourners feel the same way, only more so. Everyone attends under this leaden shroud."

"And?"

"And that's where the advertising gurus are missing a bet. Don't you see? Sell the services to the deceased before the demise! Reserve the package in advance, requiring a reasonable deposit so the home doesn't get stuck for the buffet."

"Buffet."

"Right. Or the cocktails, the band, any of those touches. You plan it, you publicize it, and obviously you attend it, though your dance card will probably remain open."

"You plan your own funeral."

"And draw a list for invitations. Who knows better which people should be there than you do? Now it's a free-for-all, gate-crashers galore. Restrict and refine, that's the ticket. Only those you really want to enjoy themselves will benefit."

"Peete, that's sick."

"Sicker than catering christenings and bar mitzvahs, weddings and anniversaries? All those events are benchmarks, my lad, benchmarks in a life. Why not a similarly anticipated blowout for the last benchmark of all?"

"The funeral homes would never go along."

"Go along? They'd jump at it! The only markups they can take now are on containers and liners. Think of champagne, pâté, and caviar. Plus the zing it would put into their commercials. No more somber dirges in the background. Instead, you'd hear some celebrity endorser announce, 'And now, for Dead to the World, a subsidiary of Out Like a Light, Inc., the largest chain of funeral spas in the East, the hard-rocking sounds of Jerry Garcia and the Grateful—'"

"Could we try something else for a while?"

Peete's features, till now theatrical, drooped back to normal. "Sorry. Always thought it was better to treat the passing of a loved one as an absurdity. Muffles it, somehow."

I raised my glass to his and clinked. "To Jane."

He nodded. "To Jane."

"You said, 'loved one' just now."

"I did?"

"Uh-huh."

"Well, I guess I did love her, in a way. You love all the new ones, you know."

"How do you mean?"

Peete lowered the drink and his voice. "The new ones come in so full of the mission, the mission that took them through journalism school and into the business itself. 'To inform and thus protect.' It takes a while for it to wear off, but on some it becomes the messiah complex."

"Liz Rendall said the same thing."

"Ah, a point of agreement between Tin Lizzy and me. I should note it for my biographer."

"You figure the complex is what Jane had?"

217

"Good sir, after enough years and cases of the hundred proof, figuring doesn't enter into it. You can almost smell it, like the scent a mother discerns from a puppy in her litter. The problem is, Jane had the fire without the emotional stability that allows some to function, indeed succeed, with and through it."

"You ever have it?"

Peete laughed. "You behold the rarest of the rare, a former addict cured of that particular affliction, though some would argue the cure is worse than the disease. Those who would so argue, however, would be wrong. Dead wrong. No, there is nothing worse than to see the world clearly and suspect, nay be certain, that you, and you alone, can improve upon it."

"Speaking of certainties, I thought you told me you never drove anymore?"

"You may have formed that impression."

"Somebody else told me they've seen your VW around town."

Peete slurped, recalled how much he liked the stuff, and drank deeper. "There are a few days, here and there, when I feel up to motoring myself about. Not many, and never at night, if Jane's death was where you were heading."

Switching off, I said, "I met with Schonsy the other day."

"Ah, and how is he enjoying his well-earned pasturing?"

"A hard man to read."

Peete gestured to the bartender, pinging a fingernail against our nearly empty bottle. To me, he said, "Tell me, which of the many faces did he turn toward your sun?"

"What?"

"Was he 'Schonsy: The meanest sonofabitch in the valley,' 'Schonsy: The counselor rabbi,' 'Schonsy: The picaresque rascal/hero,' or what?"

"Thought you said you didn't know him all that well?"

"I don't. But Schonsy is an example of a certain species, much like Jane was. I have observed other such specimens at length. Marvelous creatures to study."

"The Schonsy I saw was a battered old man, confined to a wheelchair and trying to be upbeat."

"That's what I mean. Another facet. The truly great cops can sense a scene, just like the truly great actors. They come upon a situation, and often an audience, and trot out just the right impersonation to match the circumstance."

I said, "Ida told me that Jane got her job on the *Beacon* through a friend."

"Could be. Often happens that way."

"Any idea who the friend might be?"

"No. She never said anything about it to me."

"Apparently the friend was from a Florida paper."

"That could be also. A lot of us move around in this business, Jane more than most for someone so young."

The Smirnoff arrived. I said, "You know anybody I could talk to on any Gainesville papers?"

"Singular, not plural."

"Sorry?"

"I believe you'll find Gainesville has but one daily, though God knows even the *Messenger* may have competition by now. That part of the country's gained a lot of population recently. Undoubtedly some weeklies as well."

"Yes, but do you know anybody there?"

"Probably. I've been around more than most, too. Problem is, I wouldn't remember them, and they'd think ill of me, so a letter of introduction wouldn't advance you much."

Peete drained his glass, cracking the new bottle. "Join me?"

"No. I've got things to do. Final question?"

"As many as you like. I'm not going anywhere."

"Peete, what do you think happened, really?"

Peete measured out another triple, siphoning half of it. He set the glass down. "Charlie Coyne and Jane Rust, you mean?"

"That's what I mean."

"I think a little shit living on borrowed time got knifed. I think Jane had as much to do with causing that as she did the Johnstown Flood. And, I think her blindness to her own insignificance so altered that delicate balance we all sense but refuse to acknowledge that she killed herself."

"A derelict, the one who saw Coyne get killed. He died last night."

"They often do that, drunks."

"The cops think he drowned in three inches of rain water."

"Dangerous stuff, water. Thanks for the warning."

I got up and turned to leave.

"Cuddy?"

When I looked back down at him, the boozy cheer was all gone, replaced by the leaky eyes of an old man who'd been crying hard and knew he was about to start again.

Peete said, "Allow me to reciprocate in the warning department. I told you I could smell the messiah complex? Well, my lad, you come across like you bathed in it, and I'm sick at heart from covering funerals this week."

"Thanks."

"Didn't think it would help," said Peete, lifting his glass.

I walked around Nasharbor for a while to clear my head enough for driving. In that acute accessibility to suggestion that alcohol can trigger, I realized just how sick I was of Dykestra's city "perched on the edge." Deciding to leave it, I stopped at a pay phone to call Liz Rendall to see if I could help her out by giving Ida a ride to the airport. Someone in the city room at the *Beacon* said she hadn't returned from the funeral, and there was no answer at the tugboat.

Next I tried a travel agent I knew in Boston. He said there were no direct flights to Gainesville on the weekends, but there was a seat available on the Sunday flight to Jacksonville. I could then rent a car for the seventy or so miles to Gainesville itself. I asked him to set it up, including a room for Sunday night at any motel that had a swimming pool.

Last, I dialed Nancy at the DA's office. Her secretary said she was still on the rape case. I left a message that I would see her at home that night.

"Checking out?"

"Afraid so, Emil."

Jones appeared forlorn. "Figured you might be staying on, you been here so long already."

"Not much else I can do."

He dug out my bill, worked on it with a ballpoint, then slid it over to me. "No extra charge for the message services."

Taking out three more twenties, I said, "I appreciate that. And your backing me up with Schonstein and Cronan."

"Wasn't nothing. Good to have some company I could talk to."

After counting my change onto the counter, he extended his right hand. "Stop back now, if you can."

I shook, his grasp thorny. "I will."

"Not a good week, kid."

Nasharbor didn't live up to your expectations?

"Just the opposite."

I straightened up, my left leg still stiff. Mrs. Feeney's tulips huddled against each other on the grave. The air was colder in Boston, only about sixty with a stiff breeze coming off the water. Still, it felt like heaven.

Hey, remember me?

"Sorry, Beth."

That's alright. This case really bothers you, doesn't it.

"No more than any other."

Right.

"Okay." I told her about Liz Rendall.

They say everyone has a double.

"That's not what gets me. What gets me is that I found myself attracted to her because she looked like you, not because I found her attractive. See?"

But nothing happened.

"Nothing."

John, you may have been attracted to this woman because of me, but nothing happened because of Nancy.

I didn't reply. Sometimes you get tired of telling people they're always right.

* * *

From where I was parked, I could see her before she saw me. Alighting from the red Honda Civic, she juggled a bag of groceries while shaking her key case at the front door of the three-decker.

I got out and called over. "Can I get that for you?"

Nancy turned. "Among other things."

Walking to her, I took the keys and unlocked the deadbolt. "How's the trial coming?"

"It's been rough, but we should close to the jury on Tuesday."

"Does that mean you'll have to work all weekend?"

"That means I'll have to work part of the weekend." More quietly, she said, "How are you?"

I stared at her, perhaps a little too long, because her expression grew worried. "John?"

"I'm fine now."

TWENTY-ONE

◆

The Jacksonville airport seemed a relatively small and friendly place, although it could just have been that spending Friday night, Saturday afternoon, and Sunday morning with Nancy lifted my spirits. The garment bag and I made our way to the Hertz booth.

A bronzed young woman with hair the color of honey greeted me. "How're y'all doing today?"

"Fine so far. My name's Cuddy. I believe you have a car for me?"

"One minute . . . yes, here we are. Picking up today, returning tomorrow?"

"Yes."

She leaned over the counter. "Is that all your luggage?"

"Yes."

"Well, I just had a Mustang convertible turned in two days early. Couple found they couldn't manage all their stuff in it too well. But, if you'd like, I could give it to you so long as you cross your heart you'll have it back to me by ten A.M. on Tuesday."

"I promise. Thank you."

"No trouble. Hope you enjoy it."

We did the paperwork, and she handed me the keys. "The lot's just behind us, and that there's your plate number."

I walked through the sliding doors and into the convection oven that is Florida in June.

Sweating through my shirt, I found the car, top up. The trunk was so shallow, the carryon barely fit flat. I got into the car, starting the engine and the air conditioner. Then I realized technology had passed me by.

I couldn't figure out how to put the top down.

Ten minutes later, I waved at a broad-shouldered woman in a Hertz maintenance uniform. She came over and patiently showed me the controls, including the, I thought, unfairly hidden latches at the windshield.

After brief legs on access roads and interstates, I settled onto 301, the highway southwest toward Gainesville. After the army, I'd used my last cash payday to buy a Renault Caravelle, a small, sporty car with both rag- and hardtops. Now I turned up the Mustang's radio, enjoyed the breeze raking my hair, and generally felt young and carefree.

The scenery, on the other hand, was a bit peculiar. Every other car dealer had an old Ford or Chevy impaled on a pole thirty feet high. Farm stands were selling watermelon, Vidalia onions, and boiled peanuts. There were a lot of gas stations-cum-convenience stores, the attendants wearing straw cowboy hats. Oddest of all were the pastures I passed.

Brimful of dry, yellow grass, each had a complement of gaunt cows or steers, with legions of foot-tall white birds striding on the cattle's backs.

In Gainesville, elderly white women walked with pink parasols, and elderly black women walked with black umbrellas, all raised against the afternoon glare. My Holiday Inn lay catty-corner from the beginning of the University of Florida campus. I asked the desk clerk what the little white birds were called. She said she was from New Jersey and didn't know. She did, however, recommend a dip in their Olympic-sized pool and the menu at Cedar River Seafood and Oyster Bar, just down the road. I went up to my room and changed into my trunks.

The pool area was airy and perfectly kept, the water as crystal clear and clean as the Caribbean. I swam two leisurely laps before my leg hurt, then spent a dozy hour or so lying on a chaise with a Cherry Coke and the setting sun for company.

The clerk proved stronger on food than nature. The grouper stuffed with blue crab at Cedar River was terrific, the place packed with fit, retired couples and large, young families, all seeming to enjoy immensely being in each other's collective company.

I had a screwdriver in the lounge of another hotel with a piano player so assured and mellow I stayed for two more sets and three more drinks. At 10:10 P.M., the bartender announced last call, telling me that the city required all liquor off the table by 11:00 P.M. on Sunday nights. On the way back to the Inn, bugs the size of dragonflies started smashing into my windshield, playing their own lose-lose game of Galaxians. I slowed down, which seemed to give them a fighting chance of being swept up and over the glass.

In my room, I caught most of *Ishtar* on the cable hookup and agreed that fifty-one million doesn't go as far as it used to. I fell asleep in tune with the world and about as well prepared for the next day as the lamb is for the slaughter.

Lyle Cabbiness was managing editor of the *Gainesville Messenger*. Fifty-ish and overweight, his blotchy complexion seemed unsuited for year-round sun. He was, however, happy to speak with a private investigator from Boston. I was ushered into a first-floor office with a view of the highway and an interior wall devoted to plaques and framed photos.

"Don't get many of y'all down in these parts."

"People from Boston?"

"Right, right. They say once a body spends time by the ocean, they can't endure being away from it. Most of them go down to West Palm or Lauderdale, Miami being what it is. Others try the West coast, Naples if they got the dollars. We get more the midwesterners, or old Texas hides like me. What can I do you for?"

"To begin with, what are those white birds that stand on top of the cattle?"

Cabbiness hooted. "Those? Those are egrets. Believe they call them common egrets, the crows of the South. They got a museum over to the university, you need more detail."

"No, just curious."

"Didn't figure y'all flew two and a half hours for that one."

"I didn't. I'm wondering if you can tell me something about a reporter who used to work here."

"Might, might not. Name?"

"Jane Rust."

"Ah, Janey. I remember her, indeed. What's this all about?"

"She's dead. Cops say suicide, I'm trying to . . ."

I stopped, because Cabbiness had taken off his spectacles and had rolled his rump up enough from the chair to draw a handkerchief from his back pocket. He wiped first the glasses, then his own eyes and nose. I found it a strikingly sincere gesture, and I waited until he spoke next.

"Suicide, you say?"

"Maybe."

"Janey was . . . oh, hell, worse to speak too well of the dead as too ill. Janey worked here just a summer, my first year as managing editor. She was an intern, between semesters."

"And?"

"And she, well, I guess the sociology folks would say she fell in with a bad crowd."

"How so?"

"Janey was kind of . . . impressionable. She wasn't too well formed back then, kind of looking for a role model, I guess you'd say. Unfortunately, she found the wrong one."

"Who was that?"

"Reporter here named Cassy Griffin."

"Griffin, did you say?"

"Yeah, F-I-N at the end. Born to raise hell, that one. All the time doing things she hadn't ought to."

"For example?"

"Well, we got us a little place on the West coast named Cedar Key. Kind of a resort town for this area, hour's drive. Hemingway-type bars, dockside cafes where you can see the dolphins—or porpoises, whatever y'all call them up in Boston—hunting in pairs in the harbor. Janey fell in with this Griffin, idolized her, she did, and got herself into all sorts of tight spots down to Cedar."

"Drugs?"

Cabbiness raised his chubby shoulders. "Drugs, drinking. Men, too, the wrong kind, and too many. You know much about this part of the country?"

"You mean Florida?"

"No, but that's what I mean."

"I don't follow you."

"People from up North say 'Florida,' they've got a picture in their head of Miami. Used to be beach and boardwalk. These days, cocaine and silk jackets, more likely. Gainesville now, this isn't Miami. This is the South. The Old South. Oh, the kids all go to the same schools, and everybody can eat in the same restaurants, no muss or bother. But white or black, y'all go to church on Sunday and say 'yessir' and 'nossir' and respect your elders. And a paper here can't tolerate behavior on its staff that the readers wouldn't tolerate in their homes. I let Janey finish her summer, on account of I didn't want a mark against her in the record, but I would have bounced that Ms. Griffin if she hadn't up and quit on me a week before."

"Any idea where this Griffin woman went?"

"Nope. Couldn't have cared less, either, if you get me."

"Could I look at her employment records?"

Cabbiness wagged his head. "Not even if we still had them, I'm afraid. But all the files from those days are already pitched. The paper keeps its old issues longer than its personnel files."

"Anybody still here who knew her?"

He thought about it. "No, no everybody else from those days burned out or got kicked out. By me. Oh, there might be some production people who'd remember Griffin's name, but we get a dozen folk through here a year."

"Can you describe this Griffin to me?"

"Well, let's see. She was about . . . wait a minute." He hoisted himself out of the chair and moved to the decorated wall. "Yes . . . no, no that's not her, that was . . . yes, yes, this is her, with Janey at the staff picnic that year. Catherine Elizabeth Griffin, I believe, was her full name."

I got up, joining him at the wall.

"Lordy, I did look some slimmer in those days, but then the lens, it can play tricks on you. Y'all know how they say the camera never lies? Well, don't you believe them. It can, it surely can."

The photo showed thirty or so people arranged in a mock graduation shot, half in swimsuits, half with softball outfits. Toward the center in the first row were two women, a nearly juvenile Jane Rust in a conservative one-piece, a long-haired stunner next to her in a revealing bikini, cradling something the way Davy Crockett might a Kentucky long rifle.

"That there is Cassy, the one next to Janey. She was a beauty, she was. Even with that fish-sticker."

Liz Rendall smiled back at me, the spear gun seeming a natural extension of the personality Cabbiness had described.

The midday flight back to Boston on Eastern took forever, including the serving of the "snack." When the flight attendant finally delivered the sandwich, fruit, and cookies, the elderly man next to me said, "Two different kinds of bread."

"I'm sorry?"

He pointed to his platter. "The sandwiches. The top

piece of bread's pumpernickel, the bottom piece rye. Yours, too."

I looked at my food. "I wonder why."

"Probably the robot that makes these things went on a bender last night."

It was a pretty good line, but I just didn't feel like laughing.

TWENTY-TWO

◆

At the condo, I tossed the garment bag on the bed and called Liz Rendall. The bombardier receptionist said she was on another line. I told her I'd wait.

Two minutes later I heard, "City Room, Liz Rendall."

"I'd like to speak with C. E. Griffin, please."

No response.

"I think she answers to Cassy, too."

"John, I—"

"Bullshit, Liz! What the hell do you take me for?"

"I take you for someone who understands people in tough situations."

"You'll have to do better than that."

"I will. Look, I can't talk now, not about this over the phone."

"You've already had a chance to tell me about it, and you blew it."

"John, please, you didn't know until Ida in the limo—"

"Goddammit, Liz, you knew! That's the point. You knew as soon as I asked about Hagan and Dwight Meller, and there was no bereaved aunt around then."

"You're right. You're absolutely right."

"Not to mention you could have saved me a trip to Florida."

"How about I make up for that?"

"How?"

"Dinner at my place. Tonight. Please?"

"Liz, you don't see it, do you?"

"John, I have to go. Really. Please come by. Eight o'clock. I'll explain everything then. Please?"

"Eight o'clock. It better be good."

"It will be. Bye."

I depressed the plunger and dialed Nancy's office. She was in court. I left word that I'd be back, late.

Feeling the drag effect of travel without exercise, I changed into running gear and tried to jog the river. Before I'd gone a block, the scabs on my leg from the bridge incident said they weren't ready yet. I reversed direction and walked over to the Nautilus Club.

Elie smiled till he noticed my leg. "John, what happened?"

"I fell, scraped myself up a little."

"Oh, I'm sorry. Where does it hurt?"

Pointing and flexing, I did my best to describe muscles I couldn't name. Elie took me over to a large drawing of a flayed, color-coded man's body. He helped me determine which groups I'd offended.

Retrieving my personal chart from the open file near the desk, he indicated which machines I should avoid as well as which I should use with less weight. Following the prescribed routine, I felt my body relax and my brain recover. As I was leaving, I stopped to tell him so.

"That's good, John, good. But it's not really me. It's the designer."

"Sorry?"

"The man who designed the machines, remember? I told you, he thought through every aspect of the whole system, varying each machine so it performs its own task, separate from but with the others, too."

"Give me that again."

He did. "An integrated whole. You understand?"

"I think I do. Thanks."

Back home, I showered and changed temporarily into a pair of tennis shorts. I had a sandwich and some ice water, then stretched out on the couch, mulling over a stop or two I ought to make on my way to the tugboat.

I drove up and down the streets intersecting with The Quay for ten minutes, but couldn't see any activity. Parking in front of Joe's Marine, I strolled around the back. The Alfa was behind one garage door, a soft breeze coming off the harbor. Walking to the other garage door, I peered through the webby glass. I could just see the windshield and outlines of a new black Olds. A little cute, but I had to concede there weren't many other spots to hide the car.

As I approached the dock, the tug was outlined starkly by the setting sun. I climbed the gangplank, Liz appearing at the galley door to buzz me through the gates.

Her left hand held out a wineglass. "Thank you for coming, John. Dinner can wait till after we've talked. The living room?"

I took the glass and followed her in.

She was wearing a knit blouse and stretch pants that fit her like a second layer of skin. Sinking back casually in the sectional furniture in the living room, Rendall swashed the wine slowly around the bottom of her glass. She watched me take the rattan chair, my back to the stern and ignoring my drink.

"You don't like the wine?"

"I'm sure it's fine. Just had some bad clams in Gainesville, upset my stomach."

"Oh, I'm sorry."

"Yeah. Probably you could have warned me off the place, you knew I was going down there."

"I tried to call you."

"I didn't get any messages. Answering service on the office phone, tape machine at home. Nothing."

"You must have left right after the funeral. I tried to get you at the Crestview, but Jones the Cro-Magnon said you'd checked out and hung up on me. I tried your office and home, but it's the sort of thing I couldn't leave a message about."

"Exactly what kind of thing is it, Liz?"

"You already know most of it. Or think you do, which is worse. How about you give me five minutes to tell it my way, okay?"

Recalling the chair's tippiness, I leaned back gingerly. "Go ahead."

Rendall put down her glass, positioning her body like a model for a photographer. "I was an intern on the *Beacon* the summer Dwight Meller died. Hagan and Schonsy let me get experience riding in the cruiser because they liked me, but they couldn't tell the brass about it. Well, I had a crush on Neil that was so heavy, it hurt. They were getting ready to drop me off when we all saw Meller breaking in some door. Otherwise, it was just like they said and just like I wrote. I got out of

Nasharbor to go back to Simmons, and when I graduated, I raised hell in every town that would have me for almost ten years. Pot, coke, men, so many I lost count. I was searching for something, but I didn't realize I'd already found it."

Her sincerity was hip-deep. I wondered how long she could maintain it.

"True love?"

The face hardened for just an instant, then "Yes, that's what it was. Not just a crush. Neil Hagan was the only man I ever cared for. It took me years to realize that, but I finally came to my senses. An editor in Florida named Cabbiness canned me. He tried to blackball Janey, too, just for associating with me. That's the kind of boss he was. Well, I busted out of there and out of papers for a while into a bad marriage. A real disaster, like I told you. But at least the bastard was a rich bastard, and I was set. Financially."

"But not emotionally. Spiritually."

Rendall threw her wineglass at me. It boloed crazily before shattering against the wall behind me. "I won't have you cheapen us! It was a good thing, and still is, between Neil and me."

"But just a bit outside the bonds of matrimony. His marriage, that is."

"His wife . . . his wife's been a good partner to him and mother to his kids. He can't just walk out on her. I understand that, and I'm willing to live with it. What I can't live with is never quite having Neil *and* losing my career here. I meant what I told you once, that I think I can be managing editor when they finally push Arbuckle out the door. And I'll be a damn good one, too. But none of that will ever happen if Arbuckle or anyone else on the paper can match up C. E. Griffin, intern and hellion, with Liz Rendall, professional journalist."

I said softly, "How did you ever pull it off this long?"

She seemed to dwindle a little. "The name business or the affair?"

"Both. Start with the names."

"Oh, back in seventy-one, this was a real hick paper. Lots of older reporters, been here all their lives but verging on retirement. The new ones were just coming in, baby boomers, and most of them weren't planning on the Nasharbor *Beacon* being their final rung on the ladder of success. So, by the time I came back, there really wasn't anybody I'd come in close contact with who was still on the paper. Besides, I was older. I looked different. I probably even carried myself and talked different, thanks to New York, Florida, and a bunch of stops in between."

"And the affair?"

Liz twisted her fingers in the tails of the blouse. "We've been discreet. Nobody's trying to hurt any-one."

"Not even Jane Rust?"

"I admit that was partly my fault."

"You do?"

"Yes. When Janey applied for the job, she came through the city room and, well, *she* recognized me. After all, it'd only been five years since we'd worked together in Gainesville. I thought she was kind of shaky down there, but I also thought that Cabbiness hadn't been fair to her. So, I basically maneuvered her into a spot on the *Beacon*. That's what I mean, you see? If it weren't for me, Janey never would have been here, or gotten involved with Coyne, or become so depressed she killed herself."

I lifted my wineglass as though to toast, and Rendall began to smile. Then I said, "To a marvelous performance, Cassy."

Her smile froze.

"You played me like a fish. I give you credit there. Volunteering to get information on the old Meller articles, aiming me at Dykestra and the redevelopment stuff."

"What do you mean?"

"I heard you out. Now you let me tell my version, okay?"

"John, I—"

"First, I don't see Dwight Meller pulling a B & E the way Hagan, Schonsy, and you all claim. I see poor Dwight, kind of a social outcast, getting his thrills in the alleys around The Strip, watching the ladies of the night service their customers. But the early seventies are times of change, right? Times of experimentation. Maybe a real kick for a journalism major to get it off with two cops in a cruiser."

Her features stretched, the eyes protruding.

I said, "Poor Dwight happens on the scene, and probably Hagan starts after him, to threaten him into silence, because the times they weren't quite so a changin' for the cops. But something goes wrong, I believe Hagan there, and Dwight's neck snaps. Now what to do? Concoct a story about burglary and resisting arrest, and flatten Schonsy's oft-broken nose for effect. It was a nice touch to turn you from a liability into a witness for the heroes."

"You don't know a thing."

"It gets better. Except for Dwight, everybody survives the mess. Cassy Griffin leaves Nasharbor for the fast lane, and Hagan advances, and Schonsy sort of stays the same. When you come back, Hagan sees all

238

the old virtues in the new Liz Rendall. Schonsy recognizes you, though it's no big problem, because everybody's friends and conspirators from the old days. But then, enter Jane Rust. Jane needs a job. Jane thinks you owe her one, or maybe she just appeals to you to recommend her. The problem, however, is that you never told the *Beacon* about your sojourn in Florida. Easy enough to delete from the resume. You were coming off a bad marriage, out of journalism for a while, no one's likely to ask embarrassing chronological questions that would show the Gainesville gap. But Jane, intentionally or accidentally, could do just that, especially with the name you were known by down there that somebody might remember up here with the right amount of prodding."

"Bull—"

"So my guess is you decide that getting Jane the job is the easier course, since you figure she'll foul up and get fired reasonably soon. Tell me, Cassy, did you ask Jane not to mention the *Messenger* at all? Why bring up bad times better forgotten?"

"My name is Liz. Liz Ren—"

"Still, everything's going according to plan. Hagan is looking sharp for chief, Jane according to Arbuckle is shooting herself in both feet, and you just have to wait for Neil to be anointed to get him to divorce his wife and make you two an honest couple. Not something that fits well with a candidate for chief, but not something that would get him demoted once in the top seat, right?"

She didn't reply.

"Only Schonsy's son steps in the shit. On the take from Gotbaum, and Charlie Coyne can nail him for it. Ordinarily, just a little pressure in the right places, and Schonsy Senior could fix things, get Coyne to lay off. But Coyne and Jane are into it. According to Duckie Teevens and Gail Fearey, maybe even the real thing. Real enough anyway so Coyne doesn't scare off, and now Schonsy Senior has to play his hole card. We know what that is, don't we, Cassy?"

"Don't call me that!"

"Schonsy the elder tells Hagan that either Coyne and Jane disappear, or Schonsy blows the whistle on Hagan and you, both for the Meller incident and the affair. That may ding Schonsy's influence on the force, but it is his son on the line, and convicted cops don't fare so well in state prison."

"You're saying that Neil killed Charlie Coyne and Jane Rust."

I picked up my wineglass and threw it at her. She dodged and came down seated.

"No, Ms. Rendall. I'm saying that Hagan stabbed Coyne in that alley, and that you, after not being able to sway Jane away from writing what Coyne told her, poisoned her."

"You're crazy!"

"I don't think so. The younger Schonstein is on the hook, Hagan dresses up like a bum, waits for Coyne to act in character, then knifes him in the alley behind Bun's. The problem is, that doesn't stop Jane. She was ripped up about Coyne, romantically and professionally, before and after he died. At some point she came to you, her friend from the old days. She 'idolized' you, Cabbiness said. You were the natural one she'd discuss Coyne with, both romantically and professionally. That's how Hagan and Schonsy Senior knew who the source was, to pressure first and kill later. But, like I said, Coyne's death didn't stop Jane the way you thought it would. She came to Boston, to see me. My guess is she told you about it right afterward. You were the first car her landlady heard arrive that night. The one who stayed so long. You couldn't allow a real investigation into Coyne's death. You ground up the sleeping pills, then assured Jane it was the right amount. 'Just enough to make you drowsy, Janey, so you'll fall asleep naturally.' Like maybe you did with my wine tonight."

Her eyelids flipped up and down like window shades.

"Mrs. O'Day said you were there for hours. How did it feel, Cassy, watching Jane on the couch? While you carefully searched her place for any hard evidence Coyne might have stashed. Her body would have been closing down as the powder seeped into her bloodstream. Could you hear her breathing falter? Did she make any noises—subconscious, vulnerable ones? Did you maybe, even just once, notice the photo on the dresser of you and her together?"

"You finished?"

"I am. But I'm afraid Captain Hogueira will be keeping you awhile."

"Hogueira?"

"Uh-huh. I spoke to him earlier about coming by, since what I had was a little thin for the state police. His car's parked in the garage next to yours."

A voice from the dining room level said, "That's my car, Cuddy."

I looked up at Hagan.

Rendall said, "He knows, Neil."

Hagan pointed a snub-nosed revolver at my chest from fifteen feet away. "All of it?"

Liz sounded resigned. "Enough."

My best hope was to move as Hagan came down the stairs to the living room level, but cops lead their targets and count their bullets. At that distance, it wasn't enough of a hope, so I stayed where I was as he joined us.

"Another body'll be tough to explain, Hagan, even for a police captain."

Rendall said, "Neil won't have to explain it, Cuddy. He shoots you, we take you out in the runabout a few miles, and the ocean does the rest."

"And Hogueira?"

"You told him you were coming here? I never saw you arrive."

Something danced behind Hagan's eyes. I thought about him in his office, describing the Meller incident.

I took a chance. "Neil doesn't seem to like your idea, Cassy."

She glanced up at him and saw it, too. "So *I* shoot you, John. Up close and personal, after you tried to assault me. Powder burns on your shirt, my blouse ripped, scrapings of your skin under my nails."

I forced a laugh. "They'll never buy it."

"I look like your dead wife, right? Enough to stop you in your tracks that first day at the *Beacon*. People who knew her see me, they'll buy it."

"The woman I'm seeing now. She's an assistant DA in Suffolk."

Hagan said, "Jesus."

I said, "She won't buy it."

"We'll take that chance. Give me the gun, Neil."

Hagan didn't move. I waited till Liz got impatient and turned toward him. I pushed backward off the floor hard with both feet, toppling over and tumbling against a table before I got oriented and lunged for the rear stairs.

Rendall screamed, "Shoot him! Shoot him, you idiot!"

I heard a scuffle as I climbed the stairs on all fours,

then two shots. The first splintered wood over my head. The second smacked me in the right heel, sending me sprawling at the top step. A third bullet snuffed out a light fixture at the doorway as I heaved myself through it and onto her screened porch deckside.

Hearing someone rushing up the steps behind me, I tried to use the right foot. Numb, it wouldn't support my weight, and in the near dark, I couldn't tell if I was badly hurt. I tried it anyway, crashing through a screened panel. Grabbing to break my fall, I gripped and pulled free the spear gun assembly from the gangway next to the porch.

Rolling onto my back, I nocked both slings into the notches on the metal shaft, extending just as Liz came onto the porch. She raised a hand as a shield against the setting sun and fired, the crack of the shot jolting me into pulling the trigger on the spear gun. I felt her slug thump into the bulwark behind me, but I could see where the shaft went.

Gurgling and bellowing, Liz fell to the deck and flailed wildly, the bolt through her throat, the blood cascading between her splayed fingers and onto her blouse. Hagan filled the hatchway, then dropped to his knees, helpless beside her. She was wrenching at the bolt now, the pain keeping her from pulling it free. Liz scrabbled to him, clenching the material of his pants and jacket as she tried, once and unsuccessfully, to climb up off the deck. Then she shuddered twice, and the only sound was Hagan sobbing and a car approaching, brakes squeaking on the dock below.

I edged up so I could look down on Hogueira's round face. Manos and two other officers I'd never seen before elevated their weapons to cover me.

I said, "You're a little late."

Hogueira said, "Traffic was terrible."

The two new officers clambered up the gangplank and around the gates while Manos kept his gun on me.

I said, "It couldn't be that having me dead made your case against Hagan stronger, could it?"

Hogueira pursed his lips and shrugged.

TWENTY-THREE ◆

The bullet that hit my foot put me more in need of a cobbler than a surgeon. Hogueira kept me at the station only a couple of hours. He said he thought Cardwell and the DA could wait until morning so long as I gave him my word I wouldn't leave the city. He even let me use his office telephone to make two calls: Nancy to assure her I was okay and Emil Jones to confirm a room at the Crestview.

It was about 10:45 P.M. when a cruiser took me back to my Prelude on The Quay.

He seemed surprised to see me. Not the "My God, you're alive!" look. No, more the "Gee, I didn't know you were still in town" look. We went into the living room, where he used the remote to turn off the television.

I said, "Mark doing paperwork tonight?"

"I believe so."

"And partner Cronan home sick again?"

A broad grin. "Relapse, poor guy."

"I'd tell you what happened tonight, but I'm sure you already know more about it than I do."

Schonstein resettled himself in the wheelchair, neither hand holding the Browning. "Son, I don't know what you're jabbering about."

"How about we just cut the shit and talk it out, okay? I'm not wearing a wire, and my guess is Hogueira is happy to have half a loaf in Hagan without chasing after you. So why not tell the truth, huh?"

"The truth. Why the truth?"

"Change of pace for you. I spent a lot of time this afternoon putting the pieces together and coming up with Liz Rendall, or Cassy Griffin, take your pick, and your protégé Neil Hagan. And it all worked out, except for one thing."

"Oh, and what was that?"

"Well, Hagan couldn't have gotten close enough to Jane Rust to poison her, because she didn't trust him. She practically accused him of murder in my office the afternoon of the day she died. So that made Liz the one who killed Jane."

"Never would have thought it."

"Liz might have had the strength to outwrestle a drunken Coyne and stab him, but there's no way she could have fooled a derelict who witnessed it into thinking she was a 'biggish dude.' On the other hand, the killer crawled over to Coyne, then after the tussle, got up with a knife sticking out of his leg and limped away."

"And you think that was Neil."

"No. I thought that was Neil. The problem is that in

his office last week, I brought up the Meller boy's death. Hagan was genuinely upset about it, even after all these years. What happened on the boat tonight convinced me. Hagan's paralyzed about killing. After accidentally ending Meller's life, Hagan can't intentionally take another, even somebody like me who really threatens him."

He rocked his head back and forth once. "That's very good, son. I told you once I'd have to keep my eye on you. And you're proving me right. Go ahead, finish it."

I felt an unsavory sensation of pleasure, as though I really were presenting all this to get Schonstein's professional approval. My stomach turned over. "If Hagan couldn't kill me even though I threatened him, I can't see him killing Coyne. Or searching Gail Fearey's house that night. Or trying to run me down on a bridge. Or drowning a derelict in a rain puddle."

"That last one, the bum, now that could have been an accident, you know." He rubbed his palms down his thighs, hips to knees. "Anyway, you sure can't be thinking I did those things?"

"Because of your legs?"

"That's right."

"Which is the higher retirement, regular or disability?"

Schonsy grinned.

"You took a brick in the face for your partner a long time ago. Why not a fall down some stairs for a higher pension?"

"Don't matter why I took the fall. Because of the fall, I couldn't very well do the things you mentioned."

"Oh, I'm sure you were injured. Just not as badly as some medico certified to the retirement board. You have something on the doctor? Even on the board members?"

"It's your story. You tell it."

"Disability's not a bad way of life. Just have to restrict yourself here and there around town. Take a vacation once in a while, kick up your heels at a safe distance. Plus it gives you opportunity without suspicion."

"Disability's a hard thing to live with, son. But a harder thing to take away. Especially without proof. And you haven't got any."

"I know."

"Then what do you think you're doing here? Scaring me into confessing to something I didn't do?"

"No. Just letting you know that I know. The guy who killed Coyne supposedly got up with a knife in his leg. People don't do that, the pain of the blade grating and tearing would be unbearable. But a man who wanted to cover an already existing limp could rig something. Especially a man who used to do magic tricks for kids."

"They got trick knives like that in the catalogs. Anybody could order one through the mails."

"The man who tried to run me down was an experienced driver, a professional at handling a high-speed car. Like a former cop."

"The staties get to do most of those car chases. Not us poor townies."

"The man who drowned Vip could have gotten a call from Liz, telling him I was going to meet Vip behind Bun's. That man also might know that the authorities rarely think deaths from different causes are related. Knifing, poisoning, driving, drowning, all different."

"You thinking about trying one of those 'causes' on me?"

Schonstein had managed to slip his hand under the blanket. I said, "No. No, I'd like to, but I'd never get away with it."

Schonsy sighed amiably. "Alright. What's your angle?"

"No angle. You've got a lot of juice in this town. Some of it got drained off tonight, but not so much that Hogueira's going to try to buck you, especially if Hagan just clams up."

"Neil won't say a word."

"Assume he doesn't. That means you just might have enough juice left to think about coming after me. Formally, because I killed Liz Rendall tonight, and a DA might try to make it look like more than self-defense. Or informally, like an apparently overeager mugger a month or two from now. I'm just letting you know that anything like that happens, and you and I go toe to toe. Even if you beat me, you won't come away with enough to keep Hogueira and the other wolves off you afterward."

He watched me for a solid thirty seconds. "Done."

"I wasn't offering a deal."

"Sure you were, son. And one that makes sense for both of us. Drink?"

Standing, I said no, and moved to the door.

Behind me, Schonstein said, "You know the trouble with Neil? You're right about him. He didn't have the balls to kill anybody after the Meller thing."

My hand on the knob, I said, "And you consider that a weakness, don't you?"

"Yeah, son, I do. What's eating you, though, is that you think the same thing. A flaw you know you don't share. Yes, I could have taken you a long way, Cuddy. All the way to the top."

I left before he told me more things I didn't want to hear.

The light was on in the office. I parked the car in the space for Unit 18 and walked back.

I opened and closed the door, but nobody was behind the desk. "Emil?"

His head snaked around the corner. "Sorry. Didn't hear you come in. Got the Sox on the tube. They're in Oakland, and it just started. Wanna watch?"

"I'm pretty beat. Can I just have a key?"

Jones said, "You look like hell."

He was probably right there.

"John Cuddy, you eaten anything tonight?"

I hadn't. "Don't go to any trouble."

"No trouble at all. Got some frosties in the fridge, and a couple of Sal's Depth Charge subs in the oven. Picked 'em up just after you called for the room."

I went in and sat down on and into an easy chair. It felt as though I was never getting up again.

Emil uncapped two Killian's and handed one to me. "I owe you for introducing me to these."

He adjusted the TV so that it was equally viewable from both chairs. Sinking into his, Jones said, "So, how was your day?"